The Graveyard

THE GRAVEYARD

P. M. HUBBARD

BOOK CLUB ASSOCIATES
LONDON

This edition published 1975 by
Book Club Associates
by arrangement with Macmillan London Ltd

Printed in Great Britain by
NORTHUMBERLAND PRESS LIMITED
Gateshead

CHAPTER ONE

There is an old graveyard of the Maceacherns between the road and the water where the south shore of the loch runs out in a sort of small headland. All along the rest of the shore the road keeps close to the water, but here it cuts the corner, leaving an isolated triangle of land with the road at its base and the water on the other two sides. That is where the graveyard is, stuck up among the rocks seven or eight feet above the level of the road. I do not know how they found soil enough to earth their dead in. Perhaps that is why the graves are marked by flat slabs sunk in the turf and not standing stones. There are no inscriptions. There is a dry-stone wall all round, growing up out of the rocks for all the world like a miniature Cyclopean acropolis. There is a gateway in the wall but no gate.

I know it is a graveyard of the Maceacherns, because everybody knows that, and it would not be anyone else's hereabouts. I know little else for certain. It is impossible to date it from its appearance, because as I say there are no inscriptions, and the stones are natural stones which were already weathered before they were used. Small graveyards are not uncommon in the Highlands, where you had tiny communities scattered over huge areas, and the village churchyard so familiar in the south was no feature of their lives or deaths. One story is that the people buried there are the men who died trying to resist a raiding-party of Strachans. The Strachans had come to take a wonderful red-haired woman who lived in a shieling up on the north face above the loch. She had some fancy name, I forget what. Another story is that they are the men who resisted the redcoats when they came to burn the place after the Forty-Five and got shot down for their pains. I have also been told that the dead were the victims of the great smallpox epidemic of the eighteen-forties, buried here by themselves from some half-digested notion of sanitary isolation. The last explanation, being the most practical one and the most reluctantly offered, is the most probable. As in most near-primitive places, romantic happenings are rare in the Highlands, but the romantic imagination abounds. The Maceacherns were more likely to succumb to smallpox than to resist the Strachans or the redcoats.

I used to drive past the place often enough, say once or twice a week, when I went into Kinlocheilean to shop, but I had never thought of stopping and going and looking at it. I stopped that day because there was someone there, and I had never seen anyone there before. I stopped partly because in these parts you tend to stop, or at least consider stopping, at the sight of almost anyone, and partly because of a feeling, also peculiar to the place, that if there was after all something of interest in the graveyard, I wanted to be in on it too. As it happened, I had cut the engine before I came round the bend, because there was a new rattle in the chassis I wanted to identify and could not hear with the engine running. This was pure chance, but turned out to be very important. Anyway, I ran up in neutral to a point just under the graveyard, and then I stopped the car and sat there watching the person moving about inside. I could see only her head and shoulders. I was fairly certain that it was a girl, because the hair was very fair and cut relatively short. A boy with hair like that would probably have worn it shoulder-length and a beard to go with it. And the face looked like a girl's face. At least there was no beard. After a bit she saw me watching her, and came and leant her elbows on the wall, looking down at me. It was only then it occurred to me that I had seen no other car anywhere, and I wondered how she had got there. I was still wondering this when she moved back from the wall, and a moment later she appeared in the gateway and began walking down towards me. I opened the car door and got out. I could not just sit there and let her walk all the way down. She came on, still watching me, but without any hesitation, and after a moment I started walking up to meet her. We were both serious but ready to be polite. I did not know who she was at all.

She was a nice-looking girl, not a beauty, but pretty with her fresh colouring, and a good mover in an active, springy sort of way. There were no romantic undertones in the thing at all. So far as I was concerned, she was much too young for that. But I liked her before we were anywhere near each other, and I was glad I had stopped. Also, I still wanted to know what she was up to.

I said, 'Good morning. Looking at the graveyard?' The question was as much a formality as the greeting. I knew she had been looking at the graveyard, and she knew I knew it. What I wanted to know was why, but I could not ask her that direct. She had as much business there as I had, and for all I knew more. She might be the last of the Maceacherns in search of her ancestors.

She did not sound quite like it when she spoke. Her voice seemed as much southern as mine was, possibly even more, because I had been in the glen some time now, and you need to have a very insensitive ear, or a closed mind, not to pick up some shades of the local speech. She said, 'That's right. It's a lonely place, isn't it? But very peaceful.' She

7

smiled very nicely, but she was looking me over all the time, wondering about me as much as I was wondering about her. She had heard me speak too, and she would know I was not one of the real people of the glen. I might be local gentry, because the local gentry do not use the local speech, or not to each other. For the matter of that, so might she be, but I thought if she was, I could have placed her by now, and I could not place her at all. And her voice was not quite right for that.

I said, 'It can be pretty wild later in the year.' I said that deliberately, to let her know that I lived here all the time. 'But they were used to that, presumably,' I said.

She accepted the information offered, but did not take it up. There was just a faint lift of the eyebrow. I thought she was an intelligent girl, who knew what she was up to, but was not giving much away. She said, 'I suppose so, yes.'

We had met about ten yards up from the road, but she was not going to stand there and talk. She kept on moving steadily down, and I turned and walked with her. We walked round the front of the car, and I watched her eyes and saw them turn for a moment to the number plate. It was an English registration, because I had bought the car before I had come north. I reckoned she would know this, because nearly all the Scottish numbers have an S in them. It would fill in her picture a bit, and correctly. She would place me as a southerner, who lived here, but had not been here more than a few years. In a place as empty of people and as full of personal curiosity as the Highlands, she had virtually got me identified already. Anyone would tell her. I still knew nothing whatever about her, except that she was not one of the people of the glen.

I looked round vaguely, as if I expected to find her car hidden behind a tree-stump, though of course there was nowhere you could put a car, except on the road, anywhere in sight. I said, 'I don't know—I'm driving into Kin-

8

locheilean. Can I give you a lift?'

She was still as smooth as cream and as cool as a cucumber. 'That's very kind of you,' she said, 'but don't bother. I'm not going on just yet.'

I surrendered, because there was nothing else I could do. 'Right,' I said. 'Well, I'd better be getting on.' I got into the car, and we said good-bye, and she waved pleasantly as I drove off. I got one glimpse of her in the driving mirror, standing all by herself in that vast solitude between the grey sheet of water and the hanging pinewoods of the face. I thought that the moment I was out of sight she would go back up to the graveyard. I thought that if she had heard me coming in time, she would have kept down behind the wall, and I should never have known she was there. I thought that, once I had seen her, she had, by implication, got me identified and then seen me off in the best possible order. I thought she was a cool one, all right. I still liked her, but I was a little piqued. Also I was full of curiosity. I had been in the glen too long to be wholly free of the endemic local disease.

All the same, I did not ask anyone about her. I did not mention her to anyone. I had a strong instinct not to. This was partly a natural secretiveness, which the intense, perennial scrutiny of the glen had if anything intensified. You concealed everything, however unimportant, because as long as there were unimportant things to discover about you, the glen might be slower in discovering things you did not want known. But there was more to it than that. I was sure I had been right in thinking that the girl would have kept out of my sight if she could, and that as soon as she knew I had seen her, she had come down deliberately to find out who I was. In fact, she had no reason to mind my having seen her, but she did not know this, because she did not know who I was. It seemed to follow that there was someone in the glen she did mind seeing her,

9

whether or not she knew them by sight. I had not the faintest idea who they could be, but I knew that if I mentioned the girl to anyone, her presence would have been heard of, in various forms, by everyone else in the glen in a matter almost of hours. And the thing was, whatever she was up to, I was on her side. I hope it is not necessary to repeat that in this I was not just a middle-aged man being silly about a pretty girl. I had liked her, and indeed admired her, and nothing would persuade me that either my liking or my admiration was mistaken. Whatever reasons she had for her secrecy, so far as I was concerned she was welcome to it.

She was gone by the time I got back from Kinlocheilean. I know, because I stopped the car at the graveyard and walked up to have a look. I did not stay more than a minute, because I was in a hurry to be home. I just made sure she was no longer there, and then went back to the car and drove on.

After that I waited to see if any word of her had got round. If it had, it would have reached me sooner or later. Later rather than sooner, because I was not of the glen, even though I lived in it, and things the rest of the glen knew at once could take time to filter through to me. So, as I say, I waited, but I heard nothing at all. The probability therefore was that she had got clean away with it. There was one remaining possibility. This was that not only her visit to the graveyard, but my own meeting with her there, had become known. It was a remote possibility in that setting, but anything is possible in the Highlands. There are always people around, keepers and stalkers and men with sheep on the hill, whose proper business it is to see any unusual movement on the landscape, and who are trained and equipped to do it. If I had been seen with her, and if there was some local mystery about her, then I should be involved in the mystery, and no one would mention her to me at all. As I say, it was a very faint possibility, and I hoped it was not true. But the possibility remained.

In view of what happened later, I must make it clear that I had not at this stage the least reason for supposing that the thing was of any real importance to anyone. All I knew was that, if she had been seen, this rather striking visitor to the glen at this time of the year (it was long past the tourist season and already nearly winter) would be the subject of general speculation, and that if her visit to the graveyard of the Maceacherns had been known, the speculation would have verged on the feverish. I doubt if anyone ever visited it from one year's end to another, except perhaps the occasional tourist with antiquarian interests or an eye for the picturesque. But I did not suppose that the speculation, even if it existed, would be any more than part of that all-embracing interest in other people which is a large and essential part of the glen's way of thinking.

Meanwhile I continued to speculate myself. The first conclusion I came to was that, whatever she had been up to, she had probably not been up to it alone. From the graveyard the road ran a good seven miles east back to Kinlocheilean, and an almost equal distance to the western end of the loch, where I lived. Southward there was nothing but howling wilderness and ultimately mountains. I did not think she could have walked from where I saw her, and certainly if she had walked either way along the road, she would have been seen by someone else. Indeed, I should probably have seen her myself on my way back. Excluding such fantasies as helicopters or boats on the loch (almost equally conspicuous at this time of the year), I concluded that at some time after I had left her someone had driven along the road and picked her up. The car used must have been locally unremarkable, and must have kept its exotic passenger out of sight until they were well out of the glen. The second requirement would be easy enough, but the first raised various interesting possibilities which I did not for the moment explore. Another possibility was that they had simply waited until it was dark. The dark came very early at that time of the year, and she would not have had long to wait. I knew she had not stayed in the graveyard, because I had gone up to see. But once she had concluded her business there, whatever it was, she could have walked up into the shelter of the forest trees and stayed there, watching the road, until relief arrived. That at least is what I should have done myself. It was to be presumed that the driver of the car knew where to stop for her. But the whole thing was pure speculation.

The other thing I speculated about, naturally, was what there had been in the graveyard to interest her. I had every intention of going and having a proper look at it myself, but I would not let myself do it until I was quite sure that no word of her visit had got round. So I waited a week or so, and even then I took fairly elaborate precautions. First I drove past the place, pausing just long enough to take a rough cross-bearing between a conspicuous tree on the far side of the loch and a high point on the northern skyline. Then I drove on a mile or so, parked the car at a point where I could get it well off the road, and took to the trees on the north face. When I was well up clear of the road, I turned back westwards and made my way parallel with it along the face. I could not see my shore of the loch for the trees, but I could see the far side, and could pick up my bearing easily enough when I came to it. It was rough going, and working across a slope is always more difficult than working either up or down it, but it did not take me long. When I had my bearing aligned, I turned and went straight downhill to the road. It was perfectly possible that nothing had passed on the road since I had parked my car, and in that case the whole manoeuvre had been unnecessary. I could have walked straight back along the road. But it was a risk I could not take.

As a matter of fact, a car did come along almost as I came down to the road, but I heard it coming in time. I dodged back into the trees and watched it pass. I knew who it was. It was Jim McDonach, the local builder and joiner, driving his van out west from Kinlocheilean. He had a job on at Kilstruan. I wondered what he had made of my parked car, and whether he had stopped to look for me. But at least it had not kept him. He had left it and gone on westwards, and the next time I met him I could if necessary have a story ready to account for my car being where it was. I listened carefully, heard no car in either direction and walked straight out of the trees and across the road.

It was the same grey, chilly weather as it had been when I had seen the girl here. You get a lot of it at this time of the year. It is not yet painfully cold, but it is extraordinarily cheerless. A slight breeze blew steadily from the north-west, ruffling the surface of the loch and just stirring the tops of the trees. Those were the only sounds anywhere, the water moving among the stones down at my feet and the trees moving behind me. Neither was very loud but neither ever completely stopped. I took one more look along the road and then walked up the slope and, for the second time in my life, into the graveyard of the Maceacherns.

CHAPTER TWO

The walls were higher than I had remembered, and there were stone uprights on each side of the opening. It was just as I was going through them that I was hit by a sudden wave of pure horror, totally unexpected in what had been up to then a fairly light-hearted business. I suddenly thought that the girl was there again, but no longer alive. I had a perfectly clear picture of her, very small and flat, spreadeagled over one of those grey stones. I do not know why I thought of it, except that it was a perfect place for unobtrusive death. I suppose I checked for a moment, and then fairly ran into the gateway, looking wildly to both sides of me.

She was not there, of course. There was nothing there, only the grey, lichened walls, so closely laid that no chink of light showed through them and the green turf between them. You had to look hard even to see the graves. As I have said, the stones on them were laid flat, and the turf was closing over them. There were a few islands of stone still visible among the green, but mostly you could only trace the shapes under it, so that you knew the stones were there, but would have to cut into the turf and roll it back to see them. There was no reason why you should, because even the stones you could see had no lettering on them. There was nothing anywhere to tell you anything

14

you did not already know. You knew it was a graveyard, and there, presumably, were the graves. That was all there was to see.

Once I had got over that sudden, inexplicable horror, I did not find it an unpleasant place. It was lonely, as the girl had said, but then I have a taste for lonely places, or I should not have found myself living where I was. Like so many other places in the Highlands, it could be completely transformed by a change of weather and season. On a fine day in summer, with a blue sky and the birches in leaf on the north shore, it would be just the sort of place where your visitor from the packed south thinks he would like to build a bungalow to retire to. Even now it was peaceful enough. It did not even have the nagging quality of some holy places. There was nothing particularly holy about it. I suppose some sort of service had been read over the dead at the time of their burial, but I doubt if the living had had much truck with divinity there since. And the dead, whether they had been heroes of the resistance or the victims of social deficiency, were too shadowy now to make their presence felt. They were less real now than the rocks, and much less enduring.

The actual structure, like so many of the purely utilitarian structures of unsophisticated man, was beautiful. It was not, as it looked from the road, simply rectangular, but rhomboid, tailored to the tapering shape of the tiny headland it stood on. I reckoned they had put their dead in first, and then, where the rocks were already falling away towards the water, contrived this shelter for them, bringing up stones from the shore of the loch, and piling them up from the uneven footing of the rocks with the incredibly efficient skill of the dry-stone builder, who uses imperishable gravity for mortar instead of using perishable mortar in an attempt to defeat gravity. I did not want to build a bungalow here, but I should not at all have minded being buried here, only I doubted from the look of it whether there was room for even one more grave without disturbing one of the existing tenants.

What the girl had been doing there I had not the faintest idea. She might of course have been merely waiting, but I did not think so. From the moment I saw her, I had had this impression of activity. She had been moving about, and purposefully. I even suspected that she had gone back to her activity after she had seen me off with such efficiency and charm. But there was nothing, nothing whatever, to show what she had been at. I looked over the whole place carefully, and I could not see any sign of any recent human action. I supposed that the turf could have been cut into at some point and then laid back, but you could not tell. I wished now that I had gone right up into the graveyard while she was still there, but I knew she did not want me to, and I had had no wish to do anything she did not want. I had the feeling, illogical in view of the impression she had made on me, that she might need help, but even if she did, it would be up to her to ask for it. Unless I was wrong, she knew by now where to find me. I could not think why she should come to me for help, except that I was to this very limited extent already in her secret, and she might think, from the fact that I had kept it so far, that I was to be trusted with it. I only know that I hoped she would come. I suppose the truth is that, with all my self-sufficiency, I was a little lonely, and there had been something in her that had appealed to me very strongly. But for the moment there was nothing I could do for her except go on keeping her secret.

The gateway was in the wall facing the road, and I was walking towards it when I heard a car coming from the west. What I did was only a logical expression of what was still an almost wholly illogical state of mind, but it was in the event decisive. I ducked down behind the wall and crouched on the turf just inside the gateway. That was what I thought the girl would have done if she had heard my car coming. She had not heard me coming, and I had seen her. I heard whoever it was coming, and I did not let them see me. It was decisive for both of us.

The car came on, and I crouched there, feeling the damp of the turf through the knees of my breeches, and waiting for it to pass. It was several seconds before I realised that it was not going to pass. It was slowing down, and a moment later it stopped, down there on the road immediately in front of me. I found my mouth was dry and my heart beating furiously. There was nothing there to stop for except the graveyard, and if whoever it was had stopped for the graveyard, the chances were that they would come up. And there was no possible way of escape. Of course I could have climbed the wall behind me easily enough, but not without being seen. The only thing I could do, if they did come up, was to make a show of not having been keeping out of their sight deliberately, and I did not know if I could do that with any sort of conviction. At best, if nothing serious was involved, I ran the risk of looking uncommonly foolish, and in the glen of all places I did not want to do that. At worst—but I had no idea at all what the worst might be. I could not at that stage. This was as well, or I should have been a great deal more frightened than I was.

I heard the car door open, and crawled along the wall to my right, away from the gateway. Partly I wanted to get as far away from the gateway as I could, to prolong my concealment as far as possible, and partly I was looking for a chink in the wall, so that I could get a sight of the road. There was no chink anywhere. The old builders had done their work too well for that, and the lichen and the accumulated dust of ages had done the rest. A moment later I heard voices. They were local voices, but I did not know whose. I heard them quite clearly in that slightly tempered silence. The fact that there were more than one of them made my position worse, but what they were saying gave me at once a gleam of hope.

One voice said, 'Och, I'm telling you, there's nothing there. I looked well.'

The other voice—they were both men—said, 'Had we no best go up and take another speir?'

The first voice sounded angry now. 'Och, what's the use?' it said. 'We're wasting our time, I tell you. Do you think I'd no have seen it if it had been there?'

There was a pause then, and a stronger puff of wind from across the loch blew over me in my solitary predicament and the clash of wills down there on the road below me. Whether it was the wind, or whether it spoke more quietly, I could not hear what the second voice replied when it did reply. It said something, and a moment later I heard both doors of the car shut, one after the other. For another moment the thing hung in the balance, and then I heard the engine start up. I could have cried with relief. But relief or no relief, I moved as soon as the car did. I scuttled back, still on all fours, to the gateway and put one eye round the eastern gatepost. It is one of the rules of stalking that you never look over the top of a thing when you can look round it, and even if the driver had his eyes on the road, the other might still be looking back. The car was just going round the bend before I got a sight of it, but I saw all I wanted. I knew whose car it was.

I also knew that the owner of the car would know my car when he came to it. There was not a moment to be lost. As soon as the car was round the bend of the road, I ran out of the gateway and down the slope. I took no thought now for anything else there might be on the road. I ran straight across it and up the face under the trees as

18

fast as my legs and breath would take me. I climbed to a point where I judged that, with the wind as it was, I could move fast if I had to without being heard from the road. Then I turned eastwards along the face, going slower now, and above all making sure that the road was never altogether out of sight. I wanted without fail to see if the car came back. If it did come back, I knew, after what had passed between the driver and his companion, that it would mean only one thing. It would mean that they had turned back because they had seen my car. That might indicate either a general suspiciousness or else a more positive knowledge that I was in some way involved. Either way I should not like it, but at least I had to know.

In fact I never did know. As I have said, moving sideways along a face is never easy, especially under trees, and my incessant watch on the road made it worse. I must have been most of the way back to the point above my car when I caught my foot in an uncovered root and went sprawling. I did not hurt myself or fall far. I merely came down sideways and rolled a foot or two before I fetched up against the nearest tree. But as I lay there, recovering my wits, I heard a car pass on the road below. Of course I did not see it. I could not even be sure which way it was going. I just heard the sound of the engine come up through the trees and die away again. All I could swear to was that it did not seem to be going particularly fast. It might be my two coming back for a second look, or it might be anybody going about his business along the glen. It might even be Jim McDonach coming back. There was nothing more I could make of it.

I picked myself up and went on the way I had been going. From that height I could see my car when I came out above it, and for a moment or two I stood there, peering down through the trees, trying to see if there was anyone else about. I saw nothing, and started down the face towards it. Time was important now. For better or worse, my car had been seen there, but I did not want to be seen with it, still less asked what I was doing there until I had had time to get my explanations right.

I went as quickly as I could without making too much noise about it until I was ten feet or so above the level of the road and still just under the cover of the trees. Then I stopped, motionless, with the broad foot of a tree between me and the road, to spy out the position. My ears strained for any sound of movement or voices on the breeze, and from either side of the trunk I looked over the whole ground along the road. This is a regular and almost instinctive part of stalking, this sudden freezing into immobility while your eyes, the only part of you moving, search the new stretch of ground ahead to make sure there is nothing there before you move forward into it. I say 'your eyes', because the deer are mostly silent beasts, and the insensitive human ear has virtually no part to play in finding them on the hill. But now it was not deer I was looking for. Human movements make much more noise than those of the deer, and two men find it very difficult to be together for long without saying something. For several seconds I listened and looked over every foot of ground I could see, but I saw and heard no sign of life. That was the best I could do, because I had no more time to spare. I must commit myself now. I got up from behind my tree and walked steadily but without any further attempt at concealment down to the car. Nothing stirred.

I unlocked the car and got in. It was facing east, and I did not attempt to turn it. Instead I thought I would drive into Kinlocheilean and make a show of shopping. If the car I had heard had been my two coming back, it was behind me now. If it had not, then their car would be away somewhere eastward, wherever it had been heading for when I had last seen it. I drove steadily, making as

20

much speed as the narrow winding road allowed. It was the sort of road you had to watch the whole time, especially at the blind bends, because several of the local drivers drove on the assumption that they had the road to themselves. Generally they had, but not all the time, and the narrow tarmac did not allow of much last-second manoeuvre. And once you were off it, you were in trouble, because what there was on both sides was very rough indeed, and you were fairly certain to break the car up a bit, even if you did not run square into something immovable or find yourself in the water. All the same, I drove by reflex action from what I saw ahead. With the main part of my mind I thought, because I had a lot to think about.

My first need was an explanation for my parked car. This was not as difficult as it sounds, because I was given to leaving it at all sorts of places and making off into the country one way or the other, and this was well known. I was a sort of licenced eccentric in the glen, because I did a lot of things for pleasure which most of the inhabitants did not do at all, and those that did did only because they had to to earn their living. To start with, I walked. I walked fairly big distances across country, sometimes with some particular objective, sometimes simply for the sake of walking, and I did it at all times of the year. I was what used to be called a nature-lover, only nowadays the love of nature, like so many other kinds of love, has become specialised, and you are expected, if you are going to be taken seriously, to be a bird-watcher, or a photographer, or a conservationist or something. I had no wish to be taken seriously by anybody, least of all in the glen, and I did not push the thing too far. I did watch birds, and I did take photographs, and most of all I watched the deer. But mainly I walked over the country because it was the country I had come to live in the glen for. I have not been abroad much, but so far as these islands are concerned, there is nothing in my experience remotely resembling the Highlands, and once they have got hold of your mind, the enslavement becomes total. The west coast and the islands are something else again, something much softer and more on-coming, with more than a hint of paradise in it. It is the great inland stretch of moor and mountain and glen and fresh-water loch that establishes the mastery, because it offers no sort of compromise. You take it on its own terms or not at all. There is no softness here, even in the best of seasons, and for most of the year it is very hard indeed. If you take it on, you take it on as an unaided human animal, and that is where the fascination lies. It is one of the few regions left where if you break an ankle at the wrong place and time, you can pretty well count yourself done for. And it offers more ways of breaking an ankle than most.

So I did not need much of a story to account for my leaving the car on the road and going up the north face above Loch Eilean. In fact I stopped thinking about it specifically and thought instead about the only person who seemed likely to ask me. I was still thinking about him when I got into Kinlocheilean. There I left the car in the deserted car park of the one hotel and did my bits of shopping in the few shops there were. It was only when I got back to the car that I saw I needed petrol to get me home. This was disconcerting, because there was only the one garage in the place with pumps, and I had no wish at all to go there. However, I might well see nobody but one of the hands, and I had to have my petrol. I put my shopping in the back and drove round to Davie Bain's.

CHAPTER THREE

Davie had a glass-fronted office in front of the main building, and when I pulled up at the pumps, I could see there
was no one inside it. I got out and went to look for someone to give me petrol. I was neither a tourist nor ruling-class
enough to sit in the car and sound the horn. As I came to
the open door of the workshop, the youngest of the three
mechanics (I had never known his name) came out
wiping his hands on a bit of cotton waste, and I turned
and walked with him back to the car. He put the petrol
in and I gave him the money. While I waited for the
change, I looked with the usual incredulous fascination at
the things in the display window next to the office. I have
never been able to understand why people want to embel-
lish their cars. To me a car is as strictly utilitarian as a
cooking-stove, and no one puts mascots and badges and
extra bits of chrome on his stove. Admittedly the newer
stoves have a good deal of ornamentation of their own, but
then so, heaven knows, have the cars. Even the things in
the window which pretended to a practical purpose were
not even remotely necessary. If they had been, the car-
makers would have put them on the cars to start with.
The whole display was aimed at the car-lover, not the mere
driver. It interested me just as the sex-habits of animals
and birds interested me, as something which was part of
other creatures' way of life, but which I had no urge to

emulate. The boy was still deep in his laborious calculations when I saw, reflected in the glass, a car swing in off the road and stop in the yard. I knew it, even in the glass. I did not turn, but now I was watching the reflection in the glass and not the gadgets behind it. Davie Bain got out of the car and stood for a moment, looking in my direction.

He was a big man, one of the tall, bullet-headed type you see occasionally in the Highlands. They are as different as can be from the slighter, wiry Celtic types, and I believe the physical anthropologists say they represent a much older stock, palaeolithic hunters or some such. Mostly they are gentle, easy-going people, as big men very often are, I suppose because their physical superiority has left them no need to be aggressive. But when they are not, they can be a bit nasty, and the general view, though seldom too openly expressed, was that Davie was one of the nasty ones. He was clever, too, in his way, and always on the make. He ran a very efficient garage, I think because the men who worked for him were scared of him, and steady employment in the Highlands is not a thing to be put at risk. Apart from the garage, he had a finger in a good many local pies, and in some that were not all that local. Kinlocheilean is close enough to the big road which runs from north to south across the eastern end of the glen, and the garage, being as efficient as it was, drew business from a fair distance. This gave Davie business connections well outside the glen, and where he had a connection, Davie did business, so long as there was money in it.

Like everyone else in the glen with a car, I was a regular customer of the garage, and saw Davie occasionally when I was there, but that was the limit of our acquaintance. I had the car serviced there, but I would never have bought a car from him, or for the matter of that anything else. He always treated me with a sort of fierce jocularity, which was his way of being polite. I think he recognised me as being different from the other people of the glen, of whatever class, and this made him a little wary. Now he stood there by his car, looking at me, and I wondered if he was going to come over and speak to me. I hoped he would not. Meanwhile I went on looking into the window and wishing the boy would be quick.

The boy came at last, and I turned away from the window and took the change from him. When I turned again to go back to the car, there was Davie standing between me and it. He stood there with his feet slightly apart and his hands in his pockets, looking at me with a sort of sardonic, held-in amusement which I found extraordinarily unnerving. He had a tweed deer-stalker on his big head, and his clothes altogether were a cut above anything else you ever saw in the glen, certainly several cuts above mine. They did not, even so, make him look like a townsman. He had in fact the reputation of being a highly successful poacher, and even these clothes did not make this seem unlikely. He was also, I had been told, a great piper, though whether this goes for or against a man is a matter of taste. The point was, he was a genuine man of the glen, and looked it, but he exuded a sense of affluence, and even in some way power, which made him quite different from the rest. We were both in our ways odd men out there, but I had brought my oddness with me, willy-nilly, whereas he had deliberately created his for himself. He was a formidable creature altogether.

I smiled politely into those fierce yellow eyes that looked too small in his big face. He said, 'Good morning, Mr Ainslie,' and I said, 'Good morning, Davie,' almost together. That was standard practice. Everyone called me Mister, not so much because of my class or even my age, but because I was foreign. Everyone called Davie Bain Davie, I believe even the men who worked for him, because that was what he liked being called. It went with his smile and his size. If I had called him Mr Bain, he would have thought I was trying to start something, and that was the last thing I wanted him to think. He was one of the boys, and dared you to treat him any different. We did, of course, treat him very different, and that too he liked, so long as we called him Davie and allowed him to be as ferociously good-humoured as he chose. I had never seen him turn what you would call nasty with anyone, though I was told it could happen, and it obviously frightened people very much when it did.

He did not move out of my way and I did not stop for him, but sauntered casually round him to the door of the car. 'In for the shopping?' he said.

With anyone else I should have said, 'Ay', not in a conscious effort to talk the local language, but because I had long accepted this as the normal way of saying yes. With him I made a conscious effort to be English. 'That's right,' I said. It was as if I had to assert my differentness as a counterweight to his.

He did not say anything to this, just nodded. He had moved round after me, and stood by the side of the car while I opened the door and got myself into the driving seat. He was in any case a head taller than I was, and now he looked enormous, towering over me while I set about starting the car. Then he put out one hand and rested it on the top of the door, where I had let the window down. The hand went with the rest of him, rough and red and tremendously strong, with reddish hairs flecking the back of it. When I had started the engine and was ready to move off, I suddenly saw that the hand was holding the top of the door in a tight grip. It was as if he wanted to stop the car from moving at all, and in a moment of something like panic I really believed that he could if he chose. The hand looked quite strong enough. In any case, I could

26

not put it to the test. Unless you are openly at loggerheads with a man, you cannot drive off while he is holding on to the car like that. And we were not at loggerheads at all. On the contrary, we were all smiling politeness, though on my side at least the smile was beginning to wear a little thin.

It cannot really have lasted more than a second or two, but it was profoundly disturbing while it did. Then, as suddenly as it had appeared there, the hand was taken away. He stood back and raised it in a sort of salute. Like all the rest of his social manner, it had something ironical in it, but I was not going to worry about that. I waved and smiled in return, and moved the car off, leaving him standing there. I did not look back at all. I drove into the wide part of the yard, swung the car round and set course back the way I had come. By the time I was round, he was no longer there, but I did not look to see where he was.

I turned westward at the head of the loch and took the road along the south shore. I was a little breathless and decidedly ill at ease. He had not, after all, asked me what my car had been doing earlier, parked on the side of the road a mile this side of the graveyard. I thought he almost had, but had thought better of it. Knowing my habits, there was no real reason why he should ask, but I wished all the same that he had. I did not like the idea that he might have his own explanation.

I did not even look at the graveyard when I came to it, and I was careful to keep the car moving at a steady pace as I went past it. I knew there was nothing there for me to see, but I had the feeling that there might be someone somewhere about who would see me if I stopped and got out. I had no solid reason at all for this, but it was a feeling that grew on me during the week or so which followed, and which I got used to living with. To some extent it was no more than an intensification of the feeling you always had in the glen, that everything you did was of interest to somebody, and might be used, with any degree of distortion, as evidence against you. Or even for you. I am not saying that the glen was wholly malicious, even to a foreigner like myself. There were quite a lot of people in it whom I liked, and who I felt certain, or at least believed, liked me. But they were all equally interested, because there were not very many people in the glen, and people were what, by immemorial custom, everybody was mainly interested in.

And now, as I say, I felt, or at least suspected, an intensification of this interest, because I seemed to have got myself, quite inadvertently, involved in something which was of great interest to somebody, and in particular to the one person whom, given a choice, I should have chosen not to be on the wrong side of. I did not like it, but there was nothing I could do about it, except to keep on pretending that I was not involved at all, even to the very limited and innocent extent that I was. I kept away from the graveyard, and barely looked at it when I drove past it on the road. The absurd thing was that this was exactly what I had been doing ever since I had come to the glen, up to the day I had seen the girl there, only then I had done it from sheer lack of interest, and now I did it because I was very much interested indeed.

My cottage stood on a bit of high ground near the western end of the loch, but still on the south shore. The forest that covered most of the south shore ended a mile or two east of it, and behind the cottage I had nothing but open country running up to a bare skyline. The road ran below the front of the cottage, between it and the loch, and there was a burn that went down into the loch through a culvert under the road. That was where I got my water from, pumped up into my roof tank by an electric pump which cut in automatically when the level in the tank fell to a certain point. Everyone had electricity in the Highlands. The hydro-electric scheme must have been started as a political gesture, because the amount of electricity it produced was surely farcical in relation to the capital cost, but once there it had to justify itself by getting electricity to everybody who could use it. So long as the scattered power-lines stood up, you could be very modern and comfortable, even in the middle of that wilderness. Every now and then, of course, wind or snow or a falling tree brought a bit of line down, but the hydro-electric people were always very quick about restoring it. It was only some widespread disaster that could cut off supplies for more than a day or so, and when that happened, you reverted sharply to very primitive conditions indeed. It had happened only once since I had been in the glen, and then it had been quite an experience. But in general I lived comfortably enough, and reckoned I ought to be able to go on doing so, so long as I did not get ill or develop expensive tastes. I hired no labour and did everything for myself. At some times of the year I even hired out my own labour, partly for the interest of it and partly for a little extra cash. Casual labour of this sort is very much a part of life in the Highlands, where regular whole-time jobs are in short supply and the seasonal demand for labour varies enormously. So long as I did not under-cut the going rate or keep any of the locals out of a job, nobody thought any the worse of me for it, and I possessed skills, especially out on the hill, which people were prepared to pay for.

There were half a dozen sporting estates in the glen. They divided the land between them, apart from the Forestry Commission's holdings and a few small farms on the low lands by the water. Their acreage was enormous by southern standards, but of course the land was good for nothing except the breeding of game, or forestry if the lairds had a mind to go in for it. On the whole they had not. In a country where the deer abound and the sheep run free on the hills, forestry means enclosures, and enclosures are bad for all sorts of game. The Forestry Commission, with apparently unlimited public money behind it, was always on the look-out for new acquisitions, and even in my time I had seen the dark tide of conifers creep forward a little on both sides of the glen. To the lairds the Commission was the enemy, and the owner who sold out to it was reckoned a traitor to the cause, even if the price he got was well over what he could have got from a private buyer. To the ordinary observer the trees were not the offence they can be further south, because they were at least the proper trees for the country, and the only big ones which would grow there. All the Commission was doing was in fact to reverse the mysterious natural process which at some time, nobody seemed quite sure when, had wiped out the huge natural forests which once covered much of the country. The peat hags, bare since time immemorial, are still full of enormous tree roots pickled in the bog. The spruce and larch which the Commission mostly planted were not as splendid as the native Scots pine, but at least they were first cousins to it, and commercially much more valuable. And forestry meant jobs for the locals, which except on a very small specialised scale the sporting estates did not. On balance the real people of the glen were in favour of the forestry as much as the lairds were against it. With very few exceptions the lairds were relative new-comers, people who had made their money in the south and invested some of it up here. Provided they lived on their estates and spent their money with a proper freedom, they were accepted and in some cases well regarded. The people who were resented were the ones who kept their homes in the south and opened their lodges only for the sporting seasons. It was the same sort of resentment as is felt further south for the owners of holiday cottages. The only difference was that the lodges, unlike the cottages, were useless for most other purposes, and would simply have fallen down if the incomers had not bought them.

Of the six estates four were divided two and two on either side of the loch, and the other two were at the western end, where the river ran down into it. The river, though it could be fierce in season, was not wide, and the two estates straddled it. I knew most of the lairds to pass the time of day with, and one, at my end of the glen, I knew quite well. Like the people of the glen, they did not know quite what to make of me, because I did not fit into any of the recognised categories. They spoke to me as if I was one of them, but did not invite me to their houses. This I was well content with. The lairds, like all the rest of the inhabitants, were perpetually embroiled in private wars among themselves, and I wanted no part in them. They were dominated, almost to the point of obsession, by a sense of ownership, and like everybody else they had not really enough to think about except their neighbours. Anger, like curiosity, was endemic in the glen. The country, huge, empty and impassive, towered over the human passions that pullulated at its roots, and for myself I was content to deal direct with the country.

For a week after my meeting with Davie Bain nothing happened, and I began to wonder whether I had not imagined the whole thing. If you live alone in a place like that, it is easy enough to imagine anything from murder to cancer of the liver. All the time the weather was getting colder, and at the end of the week the first snow fell. It fell thick on the high tops and thinner on the lower faces and along the water. On the low country it did not lie long, but some of the highest tops would keep their covering now until the spring. At the end of the week

31

two other things happened, just before the snow. Mr Sinclair asked me to lend a hand with his hind cull, and I saw the girl again.

CHAPTER FOUR

I had better explain, because it is something of a point of honour with me, that the annual shooting of the hinds is not sport, even though it involves many of the same activities, and needs the same skills, as the shooting of the stags, which is. Nobody is under any obligation to shoot any stags, and if they do it, they do it for sport—apart from the cash value of the carcasses, which is considerable and of course goes to the laird, whoever does the shooting. What would happen if nobody shot any stags I do not suppose anybody really knows, but the total effect on the deer population would not be great. The annual growth of the population depends entirely on the number of breeding hinds. So long as there are any stags around at all, every hind capable of breeding will produce a calf every year. If there were more stags, the competition for hinds would presumably be fiercer, and some of the big old stags might find it harder to retain their enormous harems, but the number of calves born would be the same. To control the total population, therefore, you have to limit the number of breeding hinds. That is the purpose of the annual hind cull.

There is a statutory body called the Red Deer Commission, which is charged with the duty of maintaining the Scottish herds in the best possible condition. This involves keeping down the numbers, or at least keeping them steady, especially at a time when the areas available for feeding are shrinking. The Commission has its own estimate, based on periodical counts, of the number of deer on each estate. Obviously this is pretty rough and ready, and at its best will not be correct for every day of the year, because the marches between the estates are unfenced (unless, as I have said, there is forestry), and the deer can and do move freely across them, according to the wind and the weather and the grass available. But over the year it will not be far wrong, because the deer, although they are constantly on the move, and are very fast movers, do not in fact travel very far from their own breeding grounds. A herd may divide its time between two or three estates, but it will generally be on one or the other of them. So the Commission, in its wisdom (and as far as the red deer are concerned, its wisdom may be assumed to be considerable) reckons that each laird has so many beasts, and requires him, each year, to take a fixed quota of hinds out of his herds. This is a requirement which he is bound under penalty to fulfil. He is also anxious to fulfil it, partly because it is part of a code of conduct which is the sort of obverse of his fanatical sense of ownership, and partly because the hind carcasses, too, are of steadily rising value in a world increasingly short of meat, and the money he gets for his beasts is one of the few returns he gets on the capital price and running costs of his estate.

So the hinds have to be shot; and whereas the stags are shot only by the laird and his family and friends (though usually with the incidental help of the paid hands), it is mostly the paid hands who have to shoot the hinds. It is of course skilled work, and enormously strenuous. Also, because it has to be done between late October and January, when the Highland weather is at its worst, it can be an extraordinarily cold, wet and uncomfortable business.

At any rate, it is a business I am ready to take part in if extra hands are needed, and on a big estate they generally are. The point of honour involved is this. I would not shoot the deer for sport, but when they have in any case got to be shot, and it may be, if I refuse, by less conscientious and skilful hands than my own, then I am ready to do it. And of course I enjoy it, apart from the fact that I get paid for it. If my point of honour could be seen as a quibble, I do not see it that way myself, and am prepared to stand on it.

Mr Sinclair did not bring his vintage Bentley right up to the cottage. He left it on the road below and walked up. This was understandable, because the track up from the road was a bit rough, and the Bentley was beautifully kept. I was at the sink when I saw him coming. I dried my hands and went out to meet him. It was a bright day at the moment, but very cold, with a breeze from the north-west that felt as if it had snow in it. I had not dried my hands very thoroughly, because I did not think Mr Sinclair would want to come in and I did not want to keep him waiting outside. I felt the wind catch the damp skin like flame, but there was nothing I could do about it.

Mr Sinclair was much the best of the lairds to my way of thinking. He played the part admirably and to everyone's satisfaction. Even the other lairds liked him. But he knew he was playing it. There was always this suggestion of amused detachment, as if part of him, perhaps even the main part of him, was standing aside and watching the rest of him get involved. I had an idea that he let me see this more than most people, because he recognised my own detachment. He came up the track in the pale sunshine, smiling his small clipped smile when he saw me coming down to meet him. His tweeds fitted him as naturally as a deer's skin fits the deer, and with the same casual perfection. All the same, I felt sure he thought of them as

35

something imposed on him by convention, not so much fancy dress as uniform. It occurred to me, not for the first time, that he was in all respects what you would like your commanding officer to be if you were in one of the fighting forces. I never had been, and I was pretty sure that he never had either, but it did not alter the feeling. In fact I believe he had been a professional engineer all his life, and presumably a successful one. He said, 'Good morning, Ainslie.'

By the inscrutable laws of the social system it would have been very slightly upsetting if he had called me Mister, just as it would have been very slightly upsetting if Davie Bain had not. These things are beyond logical explanation. They merely operate. By the same laws I did not call him anything. If he had been a good deal older than I was, I should have called him Sir, but he was not. I said, 'Good morning.'

'Busy?' he said. This was a sort of small standing pleasantry between us, because he always pretended to wonder what I did with my time, whereas he was almost certainly the only person hereabouts who understood.

I assumed he had a job for me, and this pleased me, because I thought I should like working for him. I said, 'Not especially.'

He nodded. 'Like to help Macandrew with the hinds? His boy can't come, and he'll need someone.'

'Yes, I'd like it very much. What have you got to get?'

'A hundred. And I don't possess one of these crawlers. You'll have to drag the beasts to the Landrover, and it's not easy dragging country, some of it. You'll have your work cut out. But the money's not bad—a lot up on last year. Of course, prices are, too. Well, that's good. I'll tell Macandrew. He'll be pleased.'

I said, 'You'll have to find me something to shoot with.'

36

He nodded. 'Have they still not given you one? Or haven't you tried?'

'Not again. It wouldn't be any use. I haven't got the qualifications.'

He gave a sort of small snort. 'Damned silly,' he said. 'There's the forestry boys get them because they're supposed to need them for their job, and all they do with them is wound other people's beasts. And there's old Grahame at the pub, with about ten acres next to the road, and never a beast on it, unless it's a piner come down to die, and he gets one, and God alone knows what he does with it. And you're a good stalker and shot, or so Macandrew tells me, and passably honest, but they won't give you one. Well, anyway. You can have mine if you like. I shan't be here much. It's open sights, though. I can't use a telescope.'

'Nor me,' I said. 'Not for the hinds, anyway. You've got to be quick.'

'Good. All right, I'll tell Macandrew you're on, and he'll let you know when he's ready to start.' He raised a hand and turned and went off down the track. Then he stopped and turned again. 'What about clothes?' he said.

I said, 'I've got all I need, I think.'

'Yes, but you won't have by the time you're finished. Especially if there's going to be snow.'

He was right, of course. All work on the hill plays hell with your clothes, and stalking worst of all, because of the amount of crawling you do. Snow makes it even worse, because dry snow crystals are about as abrasive as powdered glass. By long tradition the laird pays for the clothes his men wear on the hill, only I was not anybody's man, except temporarily, and I had to pay for my own. It was typical of Mr Sinclair to have seen the difficulty. I said, 'I think I'll need a new pair of boots anyway, if I'm going to keep my feet dry. So far as clothes are concerned, I suggest I wear what I've got and see how they do.'

He nodded again. 'Yes, all right. But bill me for replacements. I'm not trying to do things on the cheap. I want the beasts properly shot. Otherwise I shouldn't have asked you.'

'No,' I said, 'all right.' He turned again and went off down to the road. I heard the Bentley boom as I went into the house. The Bentley was not part of the act. It was not at all the sort of thing the lairds went in for. I thought it was more probably something to do with engineering.

I wondered how long it would be before I got my summons from Macandrew. I thought that would depend on the weather. From what I had seen, the beasts were still away up on the tops, but the first real snow would bring them down. This is an important consideration. Getting up to the beasts and shooting them is a matter of skill and patience, but getting them down off the hill once they are dead is sheer hard work. Once upon a time it was all ponies, but ponies have to be kept all the year round, and are getting more and more expensive to keep. Also you need a separate man to manage them, and men are getting more expensive too. There are various mechanical substitutes on the market, but none of them that I have seen will go wherever a man can go, let alone the deer, and some of them are still more trouble than they are worth. In general, you get your transport as far up the hill as you can, but to get the beast from where you shoot it to where your transport is there is still nothing for it but to put a rope on the carcass and drag it. You paunch the beast and take the head and front feet off before you start, which lessens the weight a bit, but even so it can be very hard work indeed. A well grown hind can weigh all of fifteen stone, and the going can be desperately rough. All in all, you wait till the beasts are within a reasonable dragging distance before you try to shoot them, and if you find

38

them outside a reasonable distance, you do not shoot them at all. Macandrew was an old campaigner, and I thought he would wait for the snow. Apart from bringing the beasts down, a few inches of snow make dragging much easier. But with the weather as it was there was no saying when the snow might come, and I thought I had better be ready.

As I had told Mr Sinclair, to be safe I needed new boots. In this matter of boots I was very much with the professionals as against the amateur sportsmen. If you are going to move freely on the hill at any time of the year, you must assume the probability of getting wet pretty well up to the knee. That is why all heavy clothing ends just below knee level. In this the breeches are only the natural and practical successors to the kilt. The kilt is almost certainly the more efficient, but it has got so mixed up with all this flummery about clan tartans and who can wear what, that hardly anyone now dares to wear it. At any rate, from the knee down you wear thick woollen stockings, which can be changed when you get in, or even on the hill if you choose to carry spares. The question is what to wear on your feet. The sportsman in general still finds it incumbent on him to wear heavy leather shoes, beautifully made and virtually waterproof, which are fine until he goes more than ankle deep in the bog or the burn or the snowdrift, when they immediately become walking reservoirs, guaranteed to keep his feet wet until he gets home. As he is pretty well bound to go in more than ankle deep fairly early in the day, this causes him a lot of suffering, which is presumably what he is after.

Your paid man will have none of this. In my experience the Highland stalker combines an absolute disregard for all weather conditions with a very careful regard for his own health, which seems to me an entirely admirable attitude. At any rate, he hates wet feet as he hates foxes, and like the farm worker further south, he has long since gone nap on gumboots. But whereas the farm worker merely tucks his long trousers into his boots, the stalker wears his boots under knee breeches, which are strapped up close under the knee, but because of their fullness hang out clear of his boot-tops and the stockings he wears turned down over his boots. The difference in efficiency is enormous. When the farmer's trousers get wet, they carry the wet steadily down inside his boots, until the whole leg is swathed in close-fitting dampness. With the stalker's breeches the water runs down the loose fabric into the hanging folds below the knee, and from there drips clear outside his boot leg. Even his knees are wet only when the breeches touch them, and because of their loose fit, this is only intermittent. From the knee down he can stay dry all day long in even the most horrific conditions. Of course if he gets the water in over the top of his boots, he is in a worse case even than the sportsman in shoes, but this is a disaster which can usually be avoided.

But the wear on the boots is extreme. The stalker is not just slopping about in soft mud and climbing in and out of tractors. He is walking, walking all day over some of the roughest going there is, where at every third step his boot hits weathered stone, and in between has to endure heather roots and snow and gravel and the strange spikes of pickled wood that lurk just under the surface of the peat hags. He cannot wear the heaviest quality of boot, because its weight would tire him and hamper his movements. Yet obviously the life of a light rubber boot in these conditions is a short one. And the first leak is fatal. If a sound boot will not stand up to use on the hill for long, a patch will not stand up to it at all. I had two pairs of boots, and I knew the condition of both of them precisely. If I was going to help Macandrew get in a hundred hinds, I had to start with a new pair, and that meant Aberennan, because Kinlocheilean did not have that sort of shop. To get to

Aberennan you went through Kinlocheilean to the eastern end of the glen and turned south on the main road. It was fifty miles each way, but the nearest thing I could call a proper shopping town. I decided to go that afternoon. I reckoned if I left soon after mid-day, I should be there when the shops re-opened after lunch. Even with the days as short as they already were, I ought to be just home by daylight, which I much preferred, especially if it was going to snow.

I got away very much when I planned, and the journey in was uneventful. I drove straight through Kinlocheilean and saw no one. I had enough petrol in the car to get me to Aberennan, and filled up for the return journey when I got there. Then I went in search of my boots and the one or two other odd bits of shopping which I had saved perforce for my next time in. When I had got them back to the car, it was still not quite half past two, and I decided to get some more money before the banks shut. Generally I cashed cheques at the grocers' in Kinlocheilean, and in fact if you paid your bills by cheque, a little cash went a long way in the glen, because there was next to nothing to spend it on. Not being of that sort of sociability, I did not go into Grahame's bar, but kept my own bottles in the house. However, the sight of real shops is always a temptation, and by the time I was ready to go home, I was pretty well cleaned out, so I took my cheque-book and credit card into the first bank that would honour them. It was a fine grey granite place, I remember, very solid and respectable looking, at one of the corners off the main street.

I went to one of the writing tables along the wall, made out my cheque and took it to the nearest cashier's grille open for business. There was a girl on the other side of the grille. She had her head down over some paper work, and I could not see her very clearly. I pushed the cheque and card in under the grille and waited for her to surface.

41

After a moment or two she scribbled some figure down on a slip of paper and then turned to me with the bright welcoming smile she had no doubt been taught to produce for customers, especially if you had kept them waiting a bit. I smiled back at her, as you do, automatically. I do not know which of our faces changed first, but I am sure both changed. There was no doubt at all on either side. In fact both our faces must have changed more than once, because we reacted to each other's reactions. My first reaction was pleasure, surprise of course, but pleasurable surprise, because I had liked her, and hoped to see her again, and now here she was. This did not last long, because her first reaction, apart from surprise, was apprehension. I could not be mistaken about this. It was not me she was apprehensive of, but the fact that I was there and what I might do now I was. The moment she recognised me her eyes left mine and flicked both ways, looking to see who else was about within sight of us and above all, I suppose, within earshot. There were very few people, in fact, and the whole place was very quiet, but this could cut both ways.

She had got her official good afternoon out before we recognised each other, but I had seen her dismay before I had time to reply. All these things are matters of split seconds, however many words it takes to tell them. My reaction was in fact instinctive. I gave her the most reassuring smile I could, not at all the sort of smile you normally lavish on a cashier, even a pretty one, over the cashing of a small cheque, but I said good afternoon in the most ordinary customer's voice. For good measure, I did not wait for the ritual question how I should like it, but said, 'Could I have it in singles, please?' I wanted above all, with that look on her face, to make it clear to her that I was not going to burst into reminiscences of our last meeting.

I had told myself, that first time, that she was a cool one, and in fact once the first shock was over, she recovered quickly. She said, 'Yes, certainly,' in her most pleasant business voice, but smiled a sudden, disarming, conspiratorial smile into my reassuring one. I really liked her very much. She had my name printed there on the cheque, but I do not think she needed to look at it. I reckoned she had done her homework on me long since. But there was her name, in neat gilt letters, on a little plaque at the side of the grille, because banks go in for these personal touches nowadays. It said MISS M. ALLISON, and I looked at it, and she saw me looking at it, and then we smiled at each other again. Then she handed me the money and my card back, and I took them, and we said good afternoon to each other, as pleasantly as ever, and I walked out of the bank. They must have had the doors shut for the day before I was half across the street.

I went back to the car and set off on my journey home. It was a dark afternoon already, and the skies westward had that impacted, leaden look which means only one thing. The first drifting flakes came eddying out of the dusk before I was ten miles out of Aberennan, and by the time I was into the glen it was snowing steadily. There was nothing to worry about, of course. I should be home long before the snow was deep enough to upset my driving or the wind had had time to drift it. But there is something about the first real snow of the year that is a little frightening, all the same.

CHAPTER FIVE

Macandrew came to see me next morning. Like most men
with very strenuous outdoor jobs, he was not going to walk
a step more than he need, and the Ardevie Landrover
came pounding up my track in low gear when I was thinking of making myself some mid-morning coffee. Ardevie
was Mr Sinclair's estate. It was next to me on the south
shore of the loch, and now I came to think of it, it must
include the high ground above the graveyard of the
Maceacherns, though the forests immediately above the
road were owned by the Commission. Who owned the
graveyard I had no idea. I supposed the Forestry Commission might, if its policies went down to the water, but
it might equally well be the County Council, or even one
of the churches. It did not seem to matter much.

Macandrew climbed out of the Landrover with the very
deliberate, economical movements of a man who is in perfect shape but no longer at all young. His clothes might
once have been almost as good as his laird's, but they were
much worn, and patched at knee and elbow. He wore the
plainest of tweed caps, pulled well down. He carried himself with enormous dignity, and the look on his face was
quite uncompromising, except when he smiled. He was
unlike Davie Bain in every way, but almost equally formidable. You felt he could have been the originator of all

those legendary rebukes administered by stalkers to unworthy sportsmen, and for all I know he could actually have been the originator of some of them. He had been at the game long enough, and was something of a legend in his own right. He had gone to Mr Sinclair after some tremendous row with a new-come laird further east, and the fact that he was still with him was a sufficient indication of Mr Sinclair's standing in the glen. They treated each other scrupulously as equals.

I opened the door before he got to it and said, 'Good morning, Mr Macandrew. You'll come in out of the cold?' He was too great a man for me to assume that he would wish to.

He said, 'Good morning, Mr Ainslie. Ah well, just for a minute, maybe.'

He pulled his cap off as he came in. He was quite bald except for a fringe of grey hair, and the top of his head was as weather-beaten as his face. It was a magnificent head, all the same. There was no more spare flesh on his face than there was on the rest of him. He did not sit down, and I did not suggest that he should. We stood and talked in front of the fire. He said, 'Mr Sinclair tells me you're for helping me with the hinds. Yon Colin can no spare the time from his studies.'

He said it with a sort of good-tempered disgust which he did not for a moment mean me to take seriously. His son Colin was working for his medical degree at Edinburgh, and Macandrew was immensely proud of him. I did not at all suppose that I was an adequate substitute for Colin, who had grown up on the hill under his father's eye, but I was honoured to be accepted even as second-best. I said, 'I'd like to try very much if you'll put up with me.'

'Och,' he said, 'you'll do,' and that was exactly what he meant. I still felt honoured. He stood there for a moment looking me over with a sort of benign interest. Then he said, 'Would you be for making a start tomorrow, now?'

'Any time,' I said. 'Only I may take a day or two to find my feet.'

'Ay,' he said, 'just. I thought maybe we'd go and take a look up Meall Ruadh. There'll be beasts there now with the snow down, and no too far to drag them.'

'Whatever you say,' I said. I thought that going and taking a look probably meant a hard day's work, but perhaps not too long a day.

'Fine,' he said. 'Can you be at the Lodge by eight, then?'

I said I would, and he said, 'Fine,' again, and made a move for the door.

I said, 'You'll take a dram before you go, Mr Macandrew?'

He turned and gave me an approving smile, as if he found me a promising pupil. 'Well,' he said, 'just the one.'

We had our drams and he took himself off. I had no need to make myself coffee now. Instead I thought I would walk out a little on the hill to try out the new boots. I had no reason whatever to think there was anything wrong with them, but if there was, now was the time to discover it and not tomorrow when I was up Meall Ruadh with Macandrew. There had been several inches of snow down in the night. It had stopped falling now, but the sky was still grey and there was very cold air moving from the north-west. It must be just on freezing. At any rate, the snow was not going to melt much in these conditions. Despite my plea to Macandrew to let me down gently, I knew I was in good enough shape, but several inches of snow on the hill makes for entirely different conditions, because you cannot see what there is under it. A level patch of snow may hide a sloping rock-face, and a few inches of that is enough to turn your ankle if your foot comes down on it sideways. When you can see what you are treading on, your eyes do most of the work, whatever else they are looking for, but when you cannot, you have to think with your feet. For obvious reasons it was nine months or so since I had done this, and I wanted to get the feel of it again. It was not only my new boots I had to try out.

I put myself into full working dress, even to the slim silver flask in the inside pocket of my jacket. It did not hold much, but even that could be highly restorative once the shooting was over and the dragging remained to be done. And in any sort of trouble it could be a life-saver. The only man who should never carry a flask on the hill is the man who cannot trust himself not to drink before he shoots. There are too many of those in the Highlands, but I was not one of them. The only thing I did not take was a bite of food, what the stalkers call their piece, because I was only going out for an hour or two. Whatever I carried on the hill, it was all in the pockets of my jacket, which were built for it. Anything in the way of a haver-sack can be an appalling nuisance. It is all right so long as you are on your feet, but once you have to get down, it is apt to swing into all the wrong places. Your dragging rope is carried wrapped tightly round you and your knife hung from a belt or in your breeches pocket, according to the sort of knife you favour. The only thing you actually carry in your hands is the rifle, and that is quite enough to manage. Even that is slung across your back when you start on the dragging. Now I had no rope and no rifle, and my hands were entirely free. My knife was where it always was, hanging in its sheath behind my right hip. I left my loose change on the dressing table. My notes were still in the hip pocket of my breeches, but tomorrow I would leave even those behind. You can never be sure how wet you are going to get on the hill, or in what part of you, and the small Scottish notes are soft enough without being pulped in a water-logged pocket.

I walked down to the road and turned eastwards, making for the bottom of a path that went up the face about a quarter of a mile along the road. At the first bend of the road I met Black Harry. Or rather first I met Jock, and once I had met Jock, I knew Black Harry would not be far behind. Jock was Harry's dog, a black and white creature, wary from the life he led, but surprisingly gay and friendly once he knew you. Jock came bounding up to me across the snow, and I made a fuss of him. I wished I had something to give him, but I had nothing. He was as hard as nails, with wild yellow eyes. A moment later I saw Harry himself, hatless but hung about with clothes, pushing his bicycle steadily westwards. The bicycle was hung about with the rest of his possessions. I think he did ride it occasionally, but mainly it acted as his baggage animal.

Harry was a travelling man, a gangrel. They used to call them tramps in the south, but now they hardly exist there. You have your derelicts in the cities, but they are of a different breed. They will get a roof over their heads if they can. I doubt if Harry had ever slept under a roof for more than a night or two since the time, whenever that was, that he took to the road. I had been told that the minister of some parish further east had once taken him in hand, and stripped him and washed him and re-dressed him in an old suit of his own, and tried to house-train him. But it had not lasted more than a few days. In any case, that must have been before Jock's day, because Jock was no more house-trained than Harry was, though hardly less, and not even a minister would have taken Jock on as well. You do still see people like Harry in the Highlands, I suppose because there is still room for them to live their chosen lives without upsetting other people. Once upon a time the gangrel was no doubt a thief and a poacher, because he had to live on something, but Harry lived on

48

National Assistance, which he collected regularly from one of the Post Offices. He was one of the more curious invest-ments of the welfare state, but not for my money the least worthy. He scrounged too, of course, either asking for things or picking up unconsidered trifles, but I do not think he had a police record. Nobody minded much about him either way. I had a soft spot for him because of Jock. I had had a dog of my own once, and might one day have another, only a dog is a great responsibility on the hill. All the same, I kept to windward of Black Harry. He was unimaginably filthy.

What struck you at once when you spoke to him was that he was not a local. I suppose, since he was a travelling man, there was no reason why he should be. He must have come to these parts at some time, and found what he wanted here, just as I had. I never knew what the full extent of his beat was. I assumed that, like the deer, he moved freely but over a limited area, but I did not know where his limits lay. At any rate, he was a regular visitant to the glen, and everybody knew him. He was nearly always smiling, but it was a wary, cunning smile, like Jock's. The top of his head was bald, and he had a great bulging brow, and kept the rest of his hair and beard cut to some sort of a length. That was all black. Everything about him was black except his face and the top of his head, which the weather got at. I never saw him in a hat. He came on now looking a bit like a prophet in a church window, but easier going and with a much better colour.

When he saw me, he pulled his bicycle to the side of the road and stood waiting for me. Jock came along with me, and the three of us met up together. I said, 'Good morning, Harry,' and he said, 'Good morning.' I expect he knew all he needed to know about me, but I do not think he ever called anyone by their name. He never said more to anyone than he could help. What he did say was to the point and quite clearly expressed. And his voice, as I say, was a southern voice. I am not going to pretend that he was an educated man gone wrong, or even a man with an interesting story behind him. That would have made him a romantic figure, and the Highlands are seldom romantic in fact. But he was no loony. A crack-pot, of course, but perfectly clear-headed.

He said, 'You haven't got a bit of food at the house have you—for Jock, like?' With me he always begged on Jock's behalf, never on his own. He knew that that was more likely to get something out of me, and I knew that whatever I gave him they would share on whatever scale they had got worked out between them. But in the main he was perfectly right. It was Jock I gave things to, not Harry, only I had to allow for Harry's share. If I could, I gave food to Jock direct, but you could not do this unless you caught him for a moment, as I had just now, without his master. When Harry was there, Jock would hover on the fringes of the transaction, watching eagerly, but with a wary eye on Harry. He would never have dared to take anything from me in Harry's presence.

But today I had nothing on me for either of them, and I was not going back to the house just to oblige them. They were not in that sort of need. I said, 'Och, I'm away now, Harry. Look in on your way back, and I'll find something, maybe.' I had a curious instinct to talk the local speech to English speakers, rather as you are prepared to air your French with Englishmen but shy of doing it in the presence of native Frenchmen. With the summer visitors I could be more Scots than the Scots, but of course they enjoyed it and could not tell the difference.

Harry stood there, leaning on his bicycle, and Jock stood there, wagging his tail very slightly and watching the pair of us. They both looked quite cheerful and a little crafty. Harry said, 'Going to the graveyard, then?'

I will not say my heart missed a beat, but I certainly stopped breathing for a second or two. I do not think I showed anything. I smiled at Harry in a pleasant, uncomprehending sort of way and said, 'I'm away up the hill.'

Harry smiled back. He looked more crafty than ever. I thought he had been hoping to barter a bit of charity for a bit of explanation. I also thought that if that was what he had in mind, he would try again. Then he nodded and straightened up and set off again, pushing his bicycle westwards. Jock looked at me for a moment to see if there was anything more to be got out of me. When he saw there was not, he set off after Harry and the bicycle. I watched the two of them for a moment and then went on the way I had been going. What I immediately thought of was the pile of small change I had left on the dressing table, but I did not think that would be in Black Harry's line of business. He knew the house was empty, of course, and I never locked up, but he also knew that I knew he was around. All the same, I took to the high ground at once, without waiting for the path. I scrambled across the roadside ditch and clawed my way up the stony bank above it. Once I was a little way up, I could see the cottage again. I could even see, away beyond it, the bridge where the road finally crossed the river at the head of the loch and turned north to meet the road along the northern shore. I took cover, instinctively, behind a boulder and stood motionless, watching the cottage and the bridge beyond it. Nothing stirred at the cottage, but I still waited. Then, several minutes later, I saw what I was looking for. I saw Black Harry's head and shoulders go over the bridge northward. He had made fair going, too. He certainly could not have stopped at the cottage. I left my cover and went on up the hill-face, slanting eastwards to pick up the path.

Now that I had got rid of Harry, I had time to think

about what he had said. The first thing I thought was that if Harry connected me with the graveyard of the Maceacherns, it would be because he had seen me there. He might have seen me, on any of the three occasions I had stopped there. You never knew where Harry was. Also, if anyone else had seen me there, I did not think they would have told Harry. I did not think anyone ever told Harry anything. There was no reason why they should. He himself volunteered information occasionally, if there was something he thought someone might like to know, and if he reckoned to get something out of telling them. That was the next point. If Harry had seen me at the graveyard, he might have told somebody else. If he had seen me the third time, playing hide and seek with Davie and his companion, it might well have occurred to him to tell Davie, and Davie was a man it would pay him to keep in with. I was not quite sure when he could have managed it, but I thought he could have. If he had been lying up somewhere near the graveyard and had seen me go there, he would have lain low and watched, to see what I was up to. That would be instinctive with him. Then after I had gone, he would have come down to see what there was to see, and if Davie had come back, as I thought he might have, after seeing my car, they might have met. I could imagine Davie finding Harry poking about in the graveyard and being a bit rough with him, and Harry, in self-defence, telling him about my being there. If that was what had happened, it was entirely characteristic of him that he should now think of telling me, for a consideration, what he had done. That was about the level of his cunning, opportunist but not Macchiavellian.

In any case I thought he would try again. The great thing was to hear what he had to say. In particular, I wanted to know on which of my three visits he had seen me, and whether he had seen Miss Allison. But I must not show any particular interest. I must certainly not question him and certainly not tell him anything. I had assumed, when I spoke to him, that he would come back, because he always did. I did not know how far he would go westwards, or what he would do when he got there, but I knew that at some point he would turn and start eastwards again, and I thought that when he did, he would come and see me.

My left foot came down on what must be thin ice under the snow and went six inches down into the bog beneath. I staggered and swore. I had come out to think with my feet, and I was not doing it. I put Black Harry firmly out of my mind and went on up the face.

CHAPTER SIX

Ardevie lay on the south side of the water, and there was higher ground yet, rising ultimately to fairly high mountains, beyond its southern marches. This meant that in the main it was on a north face. The very steep face above the loch, where the Forestry Commission had its plantations, must at some time have been Ardevie land, though not, certainly, in Mr Sinclair's time. But it had probably always been forest of a sort. Above the belt of trees the land rose much more gradually, but in general it continued to rise steadily towards the south, simply as part of the south side of the glen. This north-facing slope was broken in two ways. First there were two biggish corries cutting into the slope with the high rocky ridge of Sronfiadh between them. Each corrie produced its burn, and the burns joined and ran into the loch at Camusevie, coming down the steep face through the trees in what was virtually a waterfall, and was one of our tourist attractions. Second, a great rounded dome of what must have been harder rock stood out from the main slope to the west of the corries. It had a steep north face, but south of it there was no more than a shallow col before the main face resumed its southward climb. This was the Meall Ruadh. It was a great place for the deer between the extreme seasons, when they were neither down on the lower slopes close to the water nor away up on the high tops southward.

The lodge was near the western end of the estate. You got to it by a reasonable metalled road that left the main road just before it turned north over the bridge, and ran up in a left-hand curve that passed a mile or so behind my cottage. The drop to the water was much less steep here than it was further east, and there were no trees. From the lodge a track of sorts ran eastward almost the whole length of the estate. It kept more or less on the contour, passing close under the north face of Meall Ruadh and crossing the burn by a built-up ford half a mile below the foot of Sronfiadh. In most conditions you could get a Landrover the length of the track, and unless the burn was in full spate, you could always get it across the ford. If there was too much water, you left the car and crossed the burn by a wooden foot-bridge. So long as you shot your beasts not too far up the face, and could get the Landrover to the nearest point of the track below, it was mostly a reasonable downhill drag to the car, though of course the going varied from place to place. If they were in either of the corries, it was better to leave them, unless you had plenty of hands. The bottoms were full of peat hags draining into the burn, and there was much less slope to help you. From almost anywhere on Meall Ruadh you could get them down without much difficulty. I think it was that, as well as the probability that the deer would be there, that had led Macandrew to make a start there. The only trouble was the wind, which had backed a little westerly, but still had a lot of north in it. I thought we should probably take the car past the foot of the hill, and then work up its east face, pretty well across the wind, and this was what in fact we did. I had kept my expectation to myself, but it is always nice for the amateur to have his judgement confirmed in any respect by the expert.

I drove into the yard behind the lodge a few minutes

before eight, and found Mr Sinclair and Macandrew standing by the Landrover. Mr Sinclair had a rifle under his arm, and I could see another, I supposed Macandrew's, in the rack behind the driving seat. I put my car under the wall of the house and got out and walked across to them. I felt very much on trial.

Mr Sinclair said, 'Morning, Ainslie. Try this for size. It's a good little gun, I think.' He swung the rifle out from under his arm and held it out to me. I took it and found it surprisingly light compared with most of the stuff they use on the hill now. It looked a smaller bore, too. I saw it at once as the equivalent, in weaponry, of his car, vintage, with plenty of quality and no frills. I found later that the date on the barrel was in fact 1910, but rifles last longer than cars. 'It's a Mannlicher,' he said. '9.5 millimetres. A bit on the light side, but it will go through anything. You want to hit them in the right place, of course. But I'm counting on you to do that anyhow.'

I balanced the lovely, deadly thing in my hands, closing my right hand round the small of the butt and feeling for the trigger with my trigger finger. 'It's beautiful,' I said. You do not throw a rifle up as you do a shotgun, but I cuddled the butt to my shoulder and looked along the sights. The foresight was a solid blade and the backsight a wide, straight-sided V. There were no frills here, either. There was only one way to shoot with it. All you needed was to do that properly. If anything went wrong, it would be no good blaming your weapon.

Mr Sinclair said, 'Yes,' smiling a little at the way I said it. 'Like to try a shot with it before you start?'

'If you like,' I said. 'But it looks plain sailing.'

'So it is. Standard aim. Standard pull-off. Use the fixed backsight. There are leaves for longer ranges, but you won't need those for any shooting Macandrew lets you do. She'll fire flat up to any sort of a reasonable range. All right. Off you go, and Macandrew will tell me later what you've made of it.'

He and Macandrew smiled at each other over the top of my head. Mr Sinclair at least was no taller than I was, but by now I felt about fifteen and not much over five foot six.

'Ammunition?' I said.

Macandrew said, 'There's a box of bullets in the car for you. That's all you'll be needing the day. There's no need to load yet. We'll no see anything until we get up on the hill, and maybe not then.'

Mr Sinclair laughed at him. 'Get along with you,' he said. 'You'll find them all right.' He turned to me again. 'I don't expect half a dozen beasts,' he said, 'not today. I want one beast properly shot. Get on terms with the rifle first. You can go for numbers later.'

'I'll try,' I said, and Mr Sinclair nodded and went off into the back door of the lodge. Macandrew opened the driving door of the Landrover, and I went round and got into the nearside seat. Before I got in, I put the Mannlicher gently into the rack below Macandrew's rifle. He started the car and we drove off, bumping cautiously eastward along the track in the clear, grey light. We neither of us said anything at all. Macandrew kept his eyes on the track. He drove perfectly competently, but with stiff, over-conscious reactions to the machine, like a man who has been brought up with horses. Now that I came to think of it, he very likely had. I ran my window back and looked down the long slope on our left, not because I expected to see anything moving, but because I wanted to get my eyes used to the light. The snow, though it brings the beasts down, does not make for easy shooting. Unless the fall has been very heavy and the wind very light, it never covers everything on the hill. Rocks and vertical faces and even the heather ridges stand out black against it, and the alter-

57

nating black and white makes a bad background. Even if the beasts are on clear snow, the brightness makes it easy to shoot under them.

It makes the stalking more difficult, too. For one thing, the beasts can see any movement at a greater distance. I have never found any reason to believe that the deer's sight is much better than that of a long-sighted man. It is their ears and nose they rely on, and here of course there is no comparison at all. Their weakness is that if they hear anything, they try to confirm the threat with their eyes and nose before they act on it; and in normal conditions a competent stalker can hope to avoid showing himself until he is within shooting distance. On snow this is much more difficult, because his dress, like the deer's, is designed to blend with the normal colours of the hill, and stands out dark against the general whiteness. I suppose he could adopt some sort of arctic dress, but as far as I know no one in the Highlands ever does. Another difficulty is that in dry snow of any depth it is very difficult for a man to move quietly. Whatever he does, his great flat feet crunch into the crystals, and the noise it makes is quite unlike any other sound on the hill. To the scent the snow makes no difference at all. But then scent is the prime conditioning factor of all stalking, because if the deer get a scent of man, they will move without waiting for any sight or sound of him. You cannot get near the beasts at all unless the wind is blowing so as to carry your scent away from them, and you plan your whole approach on this basis. If the wind shifts, you are helpless, but so long as it holds and you are coming in from the right direction, you do not have to give it another thought. That settled, it is sight and sound that decide the thing, and in respect of both snow is on balance against the stalker.

We drove on slowly, with the dark trees now fringing the shoulder of the slope on our left and the ridged and chequered face of Meall Ruadh running up on our right. Every now and then Macandrew took his eyes off the track and had a quick look up the hill. I tried looking past him through his window, but the face went up too sharply, and from my side of the car I could not see far. I certainly saw no beasts myself. Whether he did I do not know. If he did, he did not say so. He did not say very much at all on the hill. This was a working trip, and it was no part of his duties to instruct me or enlighten me, as if I had been an inexperienced sportsman committed to his charge. All he needed to do was to get me where I could be of use to him and then see how much use I could be.

It was only when we were well past the foot of the hill and beginning to open up its eastern side that he finally stopped the car. He did not pull it off the track, let alone back or turn it. He simply cut the engine and let it come to rest where it was on the track. Then he opened his door and slithered quietly out of it. His eyes were on the hill the whole time now. I got out on my side and came round to him. I did not say anything. I could see a smallish herd of the beasts now. They were strung out along the crest of a ridge up near the top, but they looked to me a long way up the hill and uncomfortably far down wind. Whether he had seen anything more I still did not know. Finally he reached into the car behind him and brought out his telescope. He spied through it for perhaps half a minute, and then made one small, short sound. I think he said, 'Ay,' but it sounded hardly more than a sigh. He closed the telescope carefully—everything he did was care- ful now—and put it back into the car. Then he lifted his rifle off the rack and brought it out. I went round to the other side, because the butt of the Mannlicher was that way, and lifted that too off the rack and brought it round to his side of the car.

He handed me a box of ten cartridges and then spoke

for the first time since we had left the lodge. 'She'll take five under the bolt,' he said. I nodded. I was not going to say any more than I needed, either. I opened the bolt and pressed five rounds down into the magazine. Then I held the top one down against the spring while I eased the bolt forward over it. I cocked the rifle fully, turned its muzzle down towards the snow and pulled the trigger. It was a beautiful pull-off, light but quite decisive, and the sharp click of the striker pin as it came forward was about the loudest sound either of us had made since the car stopped. I put the box with the other five cartridges into the left-hand pocket of my jacket.

Macandrew was busy with his own loading, but I knew he was keeping an eye on me at the same time. He would be walking ahead of me up the face, and no one likes to walk ahead of a man, however well intentioned, who has a round in the breech of his rifle. When he was satisfied, he nodded and slung his rifle on his right shoulder. I did the same. We pushed the car doors to, holding the handles down and easing them up when the doors were shut. Then Macandrew nodded again and simply set off walking, and I fell into place behind him.

I think the quality of a stalker is shown as much by the simplicity and directness of his walk up as by the care and patience of the final stalk itself. No one can anticipate the details of the final stalk. They may depend on the precise position of the beasts themselves or on the existence, on the spot, of rocks or heather clumps or shallow folds in the ground which no one, however well he knows the hill, can know are there until he gets up to them. It is a matter of improvisation, from yard to yard, until the shooting position is reached. But the walk up is planned in advance, and depends, not on details, but on the general shape and lie of the ground. If a man knows his own ground well enough, he may carry the whole picture in his head and take his line accordingly. If he has not this enormous and detailed familiarity, he has to judge, from what he can see, how the land will lie at each point on the line between him and the beasts, and this is a matter of having an eye for the ground, which I think comes only with experience. It is one of the incommunicables, like the plasterer's eye which lets him float the plaster on to the wall by hand in a perfect vertical plane beyond the reach of screeds and spirit-levels. Macandrew had grown up in the glen, but he had come to Ardevie only towards the end of his working life, and I doubt if he really carried in his head, so far as Ardevie was concerned, the details of that tumultuously broken ground which makes up any hill face in the Highlands. But his eye for the ground was beyond comprehension. I think that at the moment he had shut his spyglass and uttered that one, hardly voiced monosyllable, he had decided what he had to do to get up to the beasts, and now he just set out to do it, and I walked after him, a few yards behind and stepping where I could in his footsteps, because the snow was already broken there and my feet made less noise.

He did not hesitate at all. The only time he stopped was when we came over a top or round a shoulder and opened up fresh ground. The one thing which your human senses cannot tell you is whether there are other beasts, which you have not seen, somewhere on the line between you and the beasts you are stalking, and if you come on them unawares, and set them running, the chances are that your beasts will see them and run too. Then in a minute or two there is not a beast left on the hill, and all you can do is to go back to a fresh start or it may be a wasted day. So you have to stop and scan every bit of fresh ground before you show yourself, and it becomes, as I have said, a matter of instinctive routine. And of course the thing cuts both ways. You may, if you are going carefully enough, suddenly find yourself within shooting distance of beasts you did not know were there, and then it is a matter of quick action to seize the unanticipated opportunity.

This time there were no surprises, or I mean not so far as Macandrew was concerned. I had simply put myself in his hands and concentrated on doing what he did. I had long since lost sight of the beasts I had seen from the car, and did not even know whether they were our target. Once as we paused I looked back, and was surprised to see how far we had come. I could see the Landrover, but it looked a very long way down. All the same, there was nothing but steady snow-covered slopes between us and it, and if we got our beasts, there need be no great difficulty in getting them down. I knew that at some point we should be under the last curve of the hill and ready to start our stalk proper. Until then I was happy to let Macandrew do the thinking.

At last we came out into a small crooked defile with a rounded knoll at the head of it. We were going much more slowly now, and stepping with exaggerated care. Somewhere under the snow the water trickled among the stones in the bottom, but that was all the sound there was anywhere. The breeze blew steadily across us, but there was nothing for it to make any noise in. At the bottom of the knoll Macandrew turned and motioned me down with his left hand. I dropped on to my knees in the snow and stayed there, while he worked his way up the slope on all fours, going slower and slower until he must just have got his eyes over the line of the top. There he froze, and I knelt at the bottom, watching him. I breathed short and quick through an open mouth and felt my heart bumping in my chest, but I did not think either was due to the climb. Finally Macandrew moved. He did not look round at all, but with his left hand motioned me sideways and forwards round the left-hand side of the knoll. He himself came back a bit and then started to work round the other side. Before he began to go forward, I saw him stop for a moment and cock his rifle, and I did the same. We did it as quietly as we could, but the two bolts made tiny answering sounds of metal on metal as they went home, bringing the top cartridge up into the breech. It is not a sound you notice much as a rule, but here it sounded immensely loud and significant. I knew that if the beasts were near enough to hear it, it would bring one or two heads up, but it was not a sound that could convey anything to them, and I thought that when it was not repeated, they would soon lose interest. Meanwhile I started to go forward round my side of the knoll, and now I was suddenly on my own.

CHAPTER SEVEN

I saw the beasts at once, as soon as I got my head round
the snow shoulder. They were along a ridge, perhaps a hundred yards ahead of us. They were grazing quietly, scraping
away at the snow with their forefeet to get at the grass
underneath, and all the time drifting forward very slowly,
the way they do, up into the wind. I could see perhaps a
dozen beasts, but I knew that there would be a lot of others
not quite in sight. There was a low ridge, with a ragged
outline of small boulders, about twenty yards ahead of us.
It was hardly more than a fold in the ground, but it intervened effectively between us and the higher ridge where the
beasts were, so that it was only the beasts on the crest that
we could see. I knew at once that the low ridge was where
Macandrew meant to shoot from. On a firing range a hundred yards is too short a distance even to be used for
competitive shooting, but on a firing range you are aiming
at a black bullseye on a light field, and the target is not
liable to move, and even if you miss the bull, all that
happens is that you score fewer points. When you are
shooting at a beast, there is no clear mark to aim at, only a
particular place in its body which you must hit, and
from the proper angle, if you are to kill the beast cleanly.
If you miss the beast altogether it does not matter, but if
you hit it in the wrong place, you may have on your hands

a wounded beast which you are in duty bound to go after and kill; and a wounded beast may run for miles, and at a pace no man can hope to emulate. No stalker worth his salt would have shot at the beasts from where we now were, and Macandrew was far and away the best stalker in the glen. What he had in mind was for us to make our way, on parallel lines, to points on the low ridge ahead, where we should have the whole herd well spread out in front of us, and at a reasonable shooting distance. But we had to get there, and if the beasts saw either of us in the process, there would not be one in sight long before we got to our ridge. It was a typical final stalk, and it was not going to be easy. I thought if Macandrew had deliberately designed a test for me, he could not have done it better, but of course he had designed nothing. The hill had had the last word, as it always does. In the meanwhile there was no time to be lost, or the beasts of their own motion might move away from us altogether, and I saw suddenly, out of the corner of my eye, that Macandrew was already on the move.

That was the last I saw of him until just before we fired. When you are stalking you watch nothing but the beasts. I slithered sideways down to the bottom of the knoll and began to worm my way forward. Snow is not bad stuff to crawl on. It is certainly much more comfortable than wet ground. The only hazard is that in moving forward you may dip the muzzle of your rifle into the snow and block the barrel. A few crystals in the mouth may do no more than spoil your shot, but a heavily blocked barrel may mean at best a ruined rifle and at worst a nasty accident. I went on, yard by yard, keeping the muzzle of my rifle up and everything else as low as possible. From where I was I could just see the backs of the grazing beasts, and their heads if they put them up, as they do from time to time as they move forward. I might have been half way across the open ground when the thing happened. There was a sudden distinct clink of metal on stone from away on my right, and all the beasts' heads came up together.

I knew what had happened. It can happen to anyone in snow. I knew that Macandrew in moving forward had caught his rifle, probably the butt, on an invisible stone, but I did not look round to see. I froze where I was, head down, flat in the snow. I waited for what seemed a very long time and then, very, very slowly, raised my head until I could just see forward between the brim of my cap and the ridge ahead. I saw what I expected to see, a line of dark heads, quite motionless, with the great ears standing up like wings on each side of them, facing our way.

If the beasts hear or see anything suspicious, that is what they do. They freeze into immobility and direct the whole battery of their powerful senses in the direction of what has startled them. Sometimes a beast will move its whole body round and sometimes it will merely swing its head round on its long neck. But it faces in your direction, with eyes, ears and nostrils all at full stretch and not a muscle moving. It may be only one or two warier beasts or it may be almost the whole herd. In any case there is nothing you can do except freeze into immobility yourself, in whatever position you are caught, and wait for them to get over their fright. It can be an unbelievably long and cold business, but it is your patience and control against that of the beasts. If you try to move at all, even to ease a cramped limb or warm a frozen hand, one of them will see the movement, and that is enough. The beast that sees you will snort and move, and the rest will move with her, and in a matter of seconds there will be not a beast in sight. I lowered my head again, a fraction of an inch at a time, and waited. For all the tension I was conscious, in a graceless corner of my mind, of an enormous thankfulness that

66

it was Macandrew who had startled them and not me.

After a bit I lifted my head again, with the same agonising slowness, just enough for one quick glimpse and then slowly down again. We were still pinned down, but several of the beasts had dropped their heads and were grazing again. I do not know how long the whole thing lasted. Even if I had thought of it, I could not have moved my arm to look at my watch. I do not even know how many times I lifted my head, and looked, and lowered it again. What I do remember is that at the end there was just one big head, towards the left of the line, which would not move and would not let us move. It was probably the beast which had first got her head up at the noise. She may even have been the only one at first to take any notice of it, with the others following suit only when they saw her at gaze. The first head up is very often the last down. It is the wariest beast of the herd, or perhaps the one which has seen something the others have not seen.

Snow is warm stuff to lie on, but if you lie in the same place too long, the snow begins to melt under you, and the chill strikes in through the damp cloth. I was very cold indeed now, and wondered how my hands would shape up to shooting if we did get up to shoot. Something, it may have been a sound, but I do not think so, made me roll my head and look sideways to my right. Macandrew was on the move again. I looked to the front and found the head had gone. I could not even see any backs now, and it could be that the single watching beast had had her way and moved, taking the rest of the herd with her. But I did not think so. A herd which has been startled and got over it is not likely to move without some fresh disturbance, and I did not think we had offered any. In any case there was no time to be lost. Suddenly free of surveillance, we both made what speed we could to the ridge.

We reached it almost simultaneously and perhaps twenty

yards apart. I made for the top under cover of a boulder on the crest, and when I looked round it, I knew the moment had come. The beasts were still there, thirty or more of them, clear in sight and many of them presenting the full flank view which is the only target you can shoot at. I picked my beast at once, a big beast near my end of the herd. For all I knew, it may have been the one which had held us up for so long. I pushed the safety-catch over and brought my rifle up. With the hind shooting there is no question of waiting for the other man to shoot. You are not there for sport. You are there to kill the beasts, and the moment a safe shot presents itself, you take it. As a matter of fact, Macandrew fired first, but only just. When I fired, I heard the thud of the impact, and my beast stood stock still for a moment, and then went down in that forward plunge which means a lethal shot. A huge sense of relief welled up in me. The truth is, I worried too much to make a good stalker. A moment later Macandrew fired again and then, after just enough time to work the bolt, a third time. I did not try for a second beast. Mr Sinclair had said one, well shot, and I had shot one well. The beasts were running now. Macandrew did not fire again, and a moment later he stood up out of the snow, and I did the same.

We both of us, almost as if we were at drill, worked our bolts, pushed the top unfired cartridge back into the magazine, brought the bolt forward over it, cocked the rifle and clicked it off at the snow. Then we started dusting the congealed snow crystals out of the front of our jackets and breeches. Only then we turned and walked towards each other.

'Well,' said Macandrew, 'you got your beast?' I nodded. 'Ay,' he said, 'I saw her go down. A big beast, a yeld hind, maybe. I saw no calf with her. I had to take the calf with mine.'

That explained his two extra shots. It is one of the rules that if you shoot a hind with a sucking calf at foot, you must shoot the calf too, because it cannot at this time of the year survive without the hind. But it is often impossible to tell, with a herd grazing together, which calf belongs to which hind. Once the hind is down, you can tell, and then it is a matter of quick shooting at the calf before it gets infected with the general panic, and runs, without the hind, to inevitable death by starvation. If you have a hind and calf clearly together, it is often better to shoot the calf first, even if it means a risk of losing the hind. The hind, on her own, will live to breed again next year. The calf on its own cannot survive. I have followed this precept on occasion and got both beasts, but most of the time you cannot be sure which calf to shoot first.

Macandrew slung his rifle over his shoulder and pulled a burnt pipe out of his pocket. He lit it, and the wind carried to me a few pungent puffs of the fierce black twist the older stalkers still smoke. 'Well, then,' he said.

We turned and walked together towards the fallen beasts. When we got near the top of the ridge, we separated, each making for his own beast. I thought even Mr Sinclair could find no fault with my shot. The wound of entry was right over the heart, and when I rolled her over, there was next to no blood on the snow under her. She had been dead on her feet before she went down. She was a big beast, as big as a well-grown stag. I was going to have my work cut out with her before I got her down to the track. There was no milk in the udder. She was a barren beast, all right. I always felt slightly relieved when I had shot a yeld hind, even if, looking at the main objective, this did not make much sense.

I did the gralloch and took off the head and forefeet. There is no use for these parts, and they add enormously to the dead weight. You leave on the hind feet until you get the beast into the larder, because you drag it from the front, with your rope taken through the skin of the neck, and the hind legs help it to tow straight behind you, rather as a sea-anchor helps to keep a boat's head to the sea. You drag the beast from the front because the natural lay of the hair is from front to back, and if you drag against it, it increases the friction with the ground, and adds appreciably to your burden. I was just getting the rope through the skin at the nape of the neck when I found Macandrew standing over me.

He was looking down at the severed head. He looked very slightly shamefaced, and this added to his huge natural dignity. He said, 'You're no taking the teeth?'

The tusk-teeth of the deer have a surprising cash value, and there are dealers who come round buying them regularly. Like the carcasses, they are mostly exported to Germany, where they are made into various sorts of rather gruesome jewellery. The teeth are stalker's perks. I said, 'No, you take them.' Then I thought this sounded rather superior, as if I was claiming laird's status, which I had not the least wish to do. 'I don't get enough of them to be worth saving,' I said.

Macandrew looked happier. 'Ay,' he said, 'just so.' He stooped and took the teeth out of the jaw with the point of his knife. He did it with a sort of lofty expertise, like a distinguished surgeon performing a very minor operation. While he was doing it he said, 'Yon Jimmy Allison, now, he was a terror for the teeth. Anybody's teeth he'd take if you no watched him.' He meant, of course, the teeth of anybody's beast. I think he was just making conversation to tide over a still slightly awkward moment, but the name caught my ear.

I got the whipped end of the rope through the two thicknesses of skin and stood up. 'Who was he, then?' I said.

'Och,' he said, 'he was a boy we had working here one season. Before your time, it was. I think Mr Sinclair took him on because yon Colonel Thompson had turned him off, and Mr Sinclair had no over-great an opinion of Colonel Thompson. No but what the Colonel had been in the right about Jimmy. No damned good he was, and Mr Sinclair turned him off at the end of the season. I told Mr Sinclair it was him or me.' He smiled at this pleasantry, and I smiled back to show my appreciation of the extravagance of it.

'Was he a local chap?' I said.

'Who, Jimmy? No, no, Aberennan man, he was, and that's where he went back to when Mr Sinclair turned him off. I heard he was in trouble later. Och, he was no good, that boy, no good at all.' He looked at the carcass at my feet. Once a beast has been paunched and had the head taken off, it suddenly looks more like butcher's meat than a dead beast, even with the skin still on. 'Yon's a big beast,' he said. 'Can you manage her?'

'I think so,' I said. 'It's all down-hill, and the snow helps.'

'Ay,' he said. 'Well, take your time. We'll get these two in and finish for the day.' He turned and went back to his own beast.

I slung the Mannlicher diagonally across my back, evened up the two ends of the dragging rope and got the rope over my right shoulder. Then I threw my weight forward and pulled. Nothing happened at all, except that the rope dug into my shoulder and very nearly had me off my feet backwards. The beast seemed immovable. I had known this happen before. It does not mean that the beast is really immovable. It means that you have not taken seriously enough the business of overcoming the initial inertia and getting her moving. All the same, it means that you have work on your hands. But then I already knew that.

I turned and looked at how the beast lay. The shoulder

71

was against a stone, not a big stone, but big enough to add considerably to the job of getting her moving. I took a short grip on the rope and lifted her forehand clear over the top of the stone. Then I let out the rope and, still facing her, leant backwards and put the work on gradually. You can pull much more strongly backwards than you can forwards, because you can pull with your arm muscles as well as using your legs and weight. Of course you cannot do it for long with a beast on the hill, because you have got to see where you are going. But for getting it moving or getting it out of a snag it is very effective. I got her moving now and over the shoulder of the slope before I turned again and took the rope over my shoulder. Then we were off on a steady slope of snow, and for a minute or two the going was fairly easy.

I was wondering about Jimmy Allison. I wondered if there was any connection between Miss M. Allison, of the Royal Bank, Aberennan, who had paid a single and apparently secret visit to the graveyard of the Maceacherns, and Jimmy Allison, also of Aberennan, who had put in one season at Ardevie, and who was no good, no damned good at all. And who had later got into trouble, though of what sort I did not know.

I did not wonder for long, because the easy snow slope ended, and I was on level ground again, where it was as much as I could do to keep the beast moving at all. It is all very well to talk of a downhill drag, but no Highland face ever offers an unbroken slope. You take, from point to point, the lowest line you can which is at all consistent with your general direction, but you cannot be going downhill all the time. I got her half-way across the level and then stopped, panting as if I had been in a fight. I was sweating, too, already under my heavy clothes. I took off my cap and scarf and stuffed them in my pockets. Then I opened my collar at the neck, got a little of my breath back and set about getting the beast moving again.

After that time went very slowly. I dragged and stopped and dragged again. The thing seemed interminable, and the damned beast seemed to develop a perverse will of her own, seeking out snags and obstacles I had not seen or thought I had avoided. But I was coming to terms with myself. I had been through it all before and knew where I was with it. As with so many hard physical jobs, I despaired after the initial effort, but gradually found that the thing could be done. I had lost sight of Macandrew altogether, but I was determined, for no good reason at all, to be down on the track before him. He would be taking his own line, no doubt, and no doubt a better line than mine, because that was a thing he could not be wrong on. Also, even if his beast was smaller than mine, he was probably taking his time. He was God knows how many years older than I was, and however well the muscles last, age inevitably saps the wind.

I came down to the track at last, and let go of the rope and stood for a moment easing my muscles and working my bruised shoulders. Then I left the beast where she was and walked off towards the Landrover. I still carried the Mannlicher, though now I took it off my back and slung it on my shoulder. Even on the total emptiness of the hill you never let your rifle out of your sight if you can help it. When I got to the car, I unloaded the rifle and put the unused cartridges back in the box with the others. One beast with one bullet. It is what you always aim at, but of course you cannot keep it up. I put the rifle in the rack. The key was still in the ignition. I knew that, or I should not have come. I backed and turned the car and started off slowly along the track. Half-way back to my beast I saw Macandrew, coming steadily down about fifty yards from the track. I stopped and waited for him, and we got his beast into the back and then went on and got mine in. I do not think I could have done it by myself, not after the dragging. We put the tail-board up, and I took my flask out of my inner pocket. I said, 'You'll take a dram, Mr Macandrew?'

He smiled radiantly. 'Och,' he said, 'you'd no make a man drink and drive?' He took the flask from me, tilted his great head back and drew an exact half out of it. Then he passed it back to me, and I drank the rest, while he got to the wheel.

By the time we had got the beasts into the larder and cleaned them and left them hanging for the dealer to collect it was nearly tea-time. Macandrew offered me return hospitality, but I wanted to get on home. The sweat was drying out of my clothes, and I was suddenly very cold again. We made our appointment for the next day, and I got into my car and went. I did not see Mr Sinclair at all.

By the time I had put my car away and got into the house, the light was already going. Even as early in the winter as this the Highland days are very short. I made sure that the water was hot and then went into the bedroom to get my clothes off. My senses were not at their brightest, and it was only gradually that I began to notice things. The pile of loose change which I had left on the dressing table was where I had left it. The folded notes, which I had left on top of my handkerchiefs in a drawer, were intact and still in the drawer, but no longer on top of my handkerchiefs. I went back into the sitting room, half undressed, and looked around. Like many people who live alone, I am systematic to a fault and have a place for everything, and I saw quite a lot of things which were not quite in their place. I shivered suddenly, and went into the bathroom and turned on the bath. As far as I could see, nothing was missing, but I knew somebody had been in the house in my absence, shifting things around.

CHAPTER EIGHT

I was too tired to do anything about it that night. For all
my telling myself that I was in fair condition, I had forgotten what getting in the hinds really did to you, at least
to start with. I had my bath and got myself some food.
Then I sat down by the fire in my dressing-gown, but I
knew at once that if I stayed there, I should go to sleep in
my chair. Even if there had been any constructive thinking
to do, I was in no state to do it. Physically there seemed
nothing I could do at all. There was very little in the
house anyone would want to steal, and nothing was locked
up. My papers, such as they were, were in the various
drawers of my desk, but there was nothing of practical
interest to anyone. Once I had counted my pound notes
and found them as many as I had left in the morning,
there was nothing else I need do. Whoever had been in
the house, he had not come to steal. He had been looking
for something, but to the best of my belief it was something I had not got. I did not think my visitor was Black
Harry. I did not know who he was. I did not know what it
was he was looking for, but I thought he had come to look
for it here because he had failed to find it in the graveyard of the Maceacherns. This was very curious, and very
interesting, and perhaps a little disturbing, but there was
absolutely nothing I could do about it. I went to bed, and

slept almost at once. But before I went to bed, I locked both doors of the cottage.

It was milder next morning, and the wind had gone full westerly, with even a bit of south in it. There had been no more snow down. What had been lying yesterday was still there, but I thought it would be thawing presently. We saw some beasts not far up on the face before we reached Meall Ruadh. They watched the car go by on the track, but did not move. Unless they are very wild, they do not mind a car much, so long as it does not stop. Macandrew did not stop. He kept the car jogging along at a steady pace until we had put a spur on the hill between us and them. Then he stopped at once, and we were out and loading our rifles in a matter of seconds. The wind presented no difficulties, and the walk up was a short one. It was only a small herd, but we got a couple of beasts and had them down to the car not much more than an hour after leaving the lodge.

It is always encouraging to get something as early in the day as this. Whatever happens now, you will not have wasted your day, and it is the wasted day which is dispiriting, though it happens often enough when conditions are difficult. As it was, I felt convinced that we should get some more, and I think Macandrew felt the same. He drove straight on to the foot of Meall Ruadh. Any beasts there were about here would have heard the sound of our shots, but it was unlikely to have disturbed them. Shooting as such does not frighten them, I suppose because the gun is too recent an invention for them to have developed an instinctive fear of it. Even a herd which is actually shot at does not run immediately. The beasts run when they see the man who is doing the shooting, which they do almost at once, because in the nature of things there must be a clear line between him and them, and if they see nothing else, they see his bolt arm working. But there are always

76

those few seconds of hesitation before they have identified the danger, and that makes it possible, if you are in a good position and quick enough with your shooting, to take two beasts out of a herd, even on your own, without risking a running shot.

With the wind as it was, there was no need to go as far east as we had the day before. We walked almost straight up the north face, but in the milder weather the beasts were further up than they had been, and were already, when we saw them, moving higher still, but slowly, grazing as they went. For all our flying start, it looked like being a long day. It must have been nearly mid-day when we came up with them, and when we did, I got two beasts to Macandrew's one. If everyone is behaving as he should, this is almost entirely a matter of luck. I got two because in the few seconds we had for shooting two beasts offered me safe shots. Macandrew killed one with his first shot, but did not fire again because there was nothing he could safely shoot at. Moreover, my shooting was not perfect, because the second beast did not go down at once, and I fired a second shot to bring her down. In fact the second shot was unnecessary. I found when I came up with her that, even hit as she was the first time, she could not have gone more than twenty yards or so. She had been hit a shade too far forward, and this may be perfectly lethal, but may not stop the heart instantaneously. It is the beast shot too far back that may go for miles before she finally goes down. But it is better to be safe than sorry, and I always tended to shoot again as long as a beast was still on her feet. In this case Macandrew would not have fired again, because he would have known from the way she moved that she would not go far. But I had not the experience to be sure of this, and I had a proper horror of wounding a beast and not killing it.

Meanwhile, we were far up on the face, and we had three

beasts to get down. Macandrew decided that we should each drag one beast a certain distance, and then leave them and both go back for the third. This was the easiest way of doing it, because each walk back gave us a breather, and with two men dragging one beast the thing is much less laborious. But it was a slow job, and by the time we had got all the beasts in the Landrover it was well into the short afternoon, and we still had five beasts to clean when we got them into the larder. This is a long and messy business, and involves taking everything out of the carcass, from the windpipe back, which you have not already taken out on the hill. The skin is left on. You work in an apron, using a hacksaw and a sharp knife. By the time we had got them all hung up, and the larder swept clean and hosed down, it was already getting dark. This time I accepted Macandrew's offer of a dram.

When we had had it, he said, 'Mr Sinclair's away south. He said will you take the rifle and look after it for him?'

I accepted this as a mark of confidence, but I knew that what it really meant was that Macandrew did not fancy cleaning my rifle, so long as it was, even temporarily, my rifle and not Mr Sinclair's. The day before I had merely left the rifle at the lodge, and I wondered who had cleaned it then. I said, 'I will, of course. I've got oil and patches, but you'll have to lend me a rod.'

'Ay,' he said, 'I've got a rod for you.'

I put the rod and the rifle into the back of my car, and drove off into the gathering darkness. I still had the box of cartridges in my pocket. It gave me a feeling of completeness. I would not attempt to explain this, except that I have a passion for rifles. I should never have felt the same about a shotgun, but then I could never shoot with a shotgun. As I crawled up the track to the cottage, my headlights picked out a motionless figure standing in front of it. It was Black Harry, leaning on his bicycle, with Jock

78

at his feet. I drove straight past him and into the garage. Even then he did not move. I had expected to see him, but not as soon as this. I was glad that I had, since yesterday, left the cottage locked.

When I came back from the garage, Jock came weaving round me, lashing himself with his tail, but Harry still did not leave the place where he was standing. All he did was to straighten up, so that the bicycle was leaning against him instead of him on the bicycle. There was nothing else for it to lean on, and he could not put it down flat on the ground, because all his possessions were hung on it. I pulled up opposite him, but well back from him, with the wind blowing across between us. I had the rifle slung on my shoulder and the rod in my hand. I said, 'Good evening, Harry.' I had wanted to see him, but I thought it was a damnable time for him to come. I was cold and wanted to get inside, but you would never ask Black Harry inside, even if he would come, which was doubtful. Jock I was sure would not.

He did not say anything at all, not even his usual line about something for Jock. He just stood there looking at me, smiling a little. It was not very dark because of the snow still about, and I could see the faint shine of his teeth and his big, protruding eyes. I thought he wanted me to ask him a question, but I was not going to. Instead I waited a moment, and then turned and went into the house. I had the key on a string round my neck, and I did not mind letting him see that. I switched on the light in the porch as I went in. Then I went through into the sitting room and switched on the lights there. I put the rifle and rod down on the sofa and drew the curtains. Then I went back into the porch, shutting the sitting room door behind me.

I had left the front door open, and when I came back to it, he had moved at last. He was standing just outside the

79

door now, still with his bicycle propped against him, so that the light fell on him. Jock had dropped into the background and stood just outside the circle of light, watching the pair of us. He had stopped wagging his tail. It was dead quiet inside and out, and there was a curious tension between the three of us. I said, 'What do you want, then, Harry? A bit of food?'

I never gave him money, and I am not at all sure he wanted it. I think he always had some on him. People said he did. What he liked was food ready to eat, preferably cooked food, because I do not think he ever did any cooking for himself, unless it was warming up tinned stuff over the stick fire he made his tea on. 'I don't mind,' he said.

I went through into the kitchen and got the remains of a meat pie out of the refrigerator. I took a knife and a piece of paper and went back into the porch with them. I had made the pie myself with ready-made pastry. It had been a good pie the first time round, but I reckoned I could spare the rest of it if I had to to get him talking. I put the pie and the piece of paper on a box in the porch, and I saw Jock's tail start to wag in the background.

I cut a slice of pie, not a very generous one, and put it on the paper. Then I straightened up and stood with the knife in my hand, looking at Black Harry. His eyes went from me to the slice of pie and back again. 'I seen you in the graveyard,' he said.

I said, 'Oh yes?' very casually, and cut another smallish slice of pie. 'When was that, then?' I put the second slice with the first and straightened up again. There was still quite a lot of pie left in the dish.

'Afternoon,' he said. 'Well, evening, really. Tea-time, like.'

I had not imagined Black Harry observing tea-time, but I suppose it is common form for late afternoon. I nodded and cut another slice of pie. I thought I had already got the thing I mainly wanted, but it was as well to be sure. I put the slice with the others and looked at him. 'Anyone else?' I said.

He looked at me suspiciously, as if I was trying to make a fool of him. 'What, there?' he said. 'There wasn't no one else.'

I put the knife down in the pie-dish and made as if to wrap up the cut slices in the paper. I could afford to force the pace now. 'When did you see Mr Bain, then?' I said. I took my hands off the paper and held them half-way between the paper and the pie-dish. I looked up at him, but did not straighten up.

'Mr Bain?' he said. He did not like this. He half turned and threw a quick glance into the darkness over his shoulder. It was a purely instinctive gesture, but very revealing.

I moved my hands back to the paper. 'That's right,' I said. 'You saw Mr Bain. When?'

He looked from me to the pie and back again. He did this two or three times, and each time he looked down the light caught the whites of his eyes, as if they were standing a little out of their sockets. At last he swallowed and said, 'Not then. Next time I come.'

I shivered violently. I was desperate to shut the door and get myself warm, but I had all I wanted. I did not say anything. I just nodded. I cut the rest of the pie out of the dish and put it with the slices on the paper. Then I bundled the paper round it and held it out to him. Jock's tail was going like a flail now. 'There you are, then,' I said.

I almost thought for a moment that he was going to leave the parcel in my hands, he was so desperate to get away, but he suddenly put out a black hand and grabbed it. It was for all the world like a stray dog, who screws up his courage to take the bit of food you hold out to him, but whips away out of reach as soon as he has got his teeth in it. Then he stuffed the parcel into the pocket of his long black coat, and was off down the track with Jock after him. They neither of them said good-bye. I shut the door and locked it, and switched off the porch light, and went into the sitting room to get warm.

I did not have a bath straight away. I was cold, but less physically exhausted than I had been the day before. Instead I made up the fire with logs filled in with bits of peat, which is one of the hottest fires I know. Then I poured myself a dram and sat down to consider things. I thought I could make out an order of events now, beginning with the girl's visit to the graveyard. First she had gone there, with some particular purpose. I had met her there, but I had not interfered with whatever she was doing, and she had presumably done it and got back to Aberennan, I did not know how. So far as I could tell, no one had seen either of us. Then, later that same day, I had stopped and gone into the graveyard for the first time. I had not stayed long or done anything in particular there, but Black Harry had seen me. He must have got there between my two visits, and been lying up in the trees. Then later, but I did not know how much later, the man I had heard with Davie Bain had gone there and looked for something but had not found it. Then I had gone there again, and had nearly been caught by Davie Bain and his companion. They had missed me on the spot, but had seen my car parked not so far away. They might or might not have gone back to the graveyard when they had seen it, but they had not seen me anywhere. Judging by his behaviour at the garage, I thought this had put ideas in Davie Bain's head, especially if he was already looking for explanations, but he had had nothing whatever to go on, and was not ready to commit himself by asking me about it. Then later again, but again I did not know how much later, Davie had met Black Harry. I thought it was probably at the graveyard, because I did not see otherwise why Black Harry should have mentioned my visit there. I thought that my earlier supposition was very likely right —that Black Harry had gone there out of curiosity, and Davie had found him there and put the fear of God into him, and Black Harry had told him of my visit partly to propitiate him and partly in self-defence. It would have been after that that someone had searched the cottage. It would have been someone in the glen, or under instructions from someone in the glen, because the glen would have known that I should be out on Ardevie with Macandrew. Meanwhile, Black Harry, seeing that something was going on, had decided to cash in on it by telling me, but had almost certainly not meant to tell me about Davie's involvement. To Black Harry's way of thinking, Davie would be a man you told things to but did not tell things about.

The question was what all this added up to, and only one explanation seemed to fit. There had been something hidden in the graveyard. I had no idea what it was, but it could not have been anything at all big. The girl had known of it, and Davie's companion, and presumably Davie himself, had known of it, but the girl had got there first. How this had happened I had no idea. So far as I knew, Davie knew nothing of the girl's visit, but he had come to know of mine, and his earlier suspicions had been reinforced. He had therefore searched my cottage, or had it searched, but had found nothing there either.

So far it made sense of a sort, but there was still an enormous amount I did not know. All I knew was that I had, in all innocence, given Davie Bain fairly solid grounds for supposing that I had put a spoke in his wheel, and it was clearly a wheel which was very important to him. I did not like this at all, and the fact that I could not, even if I wanted to, tell him anything more made it worse, be-

83

cause he would not believe me if I said so. Not, that is, unless I told him about the girl, which of course I had no intention of doing.

I thought Miss M. Allison, of the Royal Bank at Aberennan, was very charming, and very cool, and probably very clever, but she had got me into a bit of a mess all the same. The fact that she had certainly had no intention of doing anything of the sort, and presumably did not know she had, did not help. The truth is that I was afraid of Davie Bain, as I thought quite a lot of people were, Black Harry for one. What I could do about it was another matter. The only person who could clear things up at all was the girl herself. I did not want to do anything that might get her further involved, but there was another side to it. It seemed to be true that Davie did not know of her visit to the graveyard, but for all I knew—and I knew so little —he might have other grounds for thinking she was involved, whereas she might have none for thinking he was. If that was so, it was high time somebody told her. On the whole I thought that, unless something happened to clear things up a bit, I might drive into Aberennan one of these days and have a word with Miss Allison.

In the meantime, it gave me more than a little satisfaction to know that I had that wicked little rifle and a box of cartridges in the house. I did not really think it would come to physical violence, but Davie was a lot bigger and stronger than I was. A high-velocity sporting rifle is not the ideal weapon for self-defence, but it is better than nothing.

That reminded me of my last duty for the day. I cleaned the Mannlicher lovingly and locked it up in my wardrobe, which I did not normally keep locked, and put the key in my pocket. Then I had my supper and a bath and went to bed.

CHAPTER NINE

By the next morning most of the snow had gone, and the
wind was a mild westerly with a hint of rain in it. The
beasts were further up than ever, and we did a long stalk
up the east face of Sronfiadh, and shot two right on the
crest of the ridge. I brought my beast down with my first
shot, and could almost certainly have had a second, but
did not fire again. I knew too well what would be involved
if I did. Macandrew fired twice, but got only the one beast.
I did not know whether he had fired a second shot at the
beast he had killed, or whether he had tried for another
and had a clean miss. I thought the first, because he would
have had the same thing in mind as I had. Needless to
say, I did not ask.

So we had our two beasts right on the top of Sronfiadh,
and well southward along the ridge, and we had enough
on our hands to get them down, without having to go back
for more. Eastward and westward of us the hill went down
sharply within no distance at all, but if we had gone either
way, we should have landed ourselves and our beasts in
the almost level peat-hags of one corrie or the other, and
they make bad enough going if you are on your own, without a dead beast bumping and splashing along behind you,
hooking itself into every snag the way they do. The only
thing to do was to drag them all the way back along the
top of the ridge and then down the more gradual slope of
the north face. Even then we should have quite a long

drag to the track, and one burn or the other to cross before we got there. It would be a fair day's work by the time we finished, even with only two beasts to clean when we got in, and with our five the day before we should be averaging three a day, which was steady enough.

That was a Thursday, and when we had finished, I asked Macandrew if I could have the next day off. There was no money involved, because Mr Sinclair would be paying me by the day anyhow. It was just a matter of convenience and keeping up with the job. I did not know whether he would want to go out on the Saturday, but I was ready to go if he did. No one ever shoots on a Sunday, except of course the poachers, who are mostly otherwise occupied during the week, and hope that on Sunday the keeper will have his feet up by the fire. I wanted Friday because I did not know how to get in touch with Miss Allison except at the bank, and whatever bankers do on a Saturday, they no longer admit the public to see them doing it.

Macandrew raised a gingery eyebrow, as he always did when he was embarking on one of his regal pleasantries, and said, 'What, have I been over-working you, man?' He had long since stopped calling me Mr Ainslie, though I still called him Mr Macandrew if I called him anything at all.

I laughed pleasantly and said no, it wasn't that, but I had business at the bank, and Saturday would not do. I never believe in telling more lies than I can help, in however good a cause, and in any case there are a lot of banks around, even in the Highlands.

'Ay,' he said, 'well. Maybe it will do no harm to leave the beasts rest for a day. Or maybe I'll go out myself. Will you be for going out on Saturday, then?'

'I can,' I said, 'certainly.'

'Ay, well I'm no so sure whether I will, but you'll no

mind doing a day on your own?' He gave his regal smile again. 'Now I know you're to be trusted,' he said.

'I'd not mind at all,' I said. In point of fact I knew I should enjoy it very much indeed. This was no reflection on Macandrew, but solitude in all the occupations of the hill doubles their fascination. All the same, I did not say so.

'Well,' he said, 'do you come on Saturday morning, and we'll see how it's to be.' We left it at that. Nothing happened that evening to change my plans, and the next morning I set off early for Aberennan.

I had no need to stop in Kinlocheilean, and certainly no wish to. I went by the south shore of the loch, past the graveyard of the Maceacherns, but did not so much as look at it as I went past. In any case, I thought it was no longer the centre of any particular attention. If I was right about the order of events, there had been nothing there, even the first time I went into it, of more recent interest than the long-dead Maceacherns. Whatever had been there, it was now somewhere else, and presumably only Miss Allison knew where.

When I got to the eastern end of the loch, I drove straight on for the main road to Aberennan. This did not involve passing Davie Bain's garage. I saw a few people on the outskirts of the village, but no one I knew by sight. Even so, I had a fancy to see if there was any local car on the road behind me, and a few miles out I turned sharply off the road and pulled the car into a forestry gate that was standing open. I waited a few minutes, but nothing passed on the road in either direction, and I backed the car out and drove on again. All this hide-and-seek made me wonder whether I was not over-dramatising the whole thing, but I had the girl to consider, and told myself that it was better to take it too seriously than not seriously enough. I had, after all, been the object of a criminal act, if walking into an unlocked house and having a look round was a criminal act, which I was not sure of. The only other precaution I took was that when I had parked the car and walked to the bank, I went past it on the other side of the street, trying to see if there was anyone who could conceivably be suspected of hanging about and watching it. I am no expert in such matters, but as far as I could tell, no one was. Aberennan is on the whole a cheerful, bustling place and everyone I saw seemed to be bustling as cheerfully as ever. I went into a shop to justify my coming that way, and then walked straight back to the bank. As I came to it, I pulled my cheque-book and credit card out of my pocket. I went into the bank holding them in my hand, and went straight to one of the writing desks along the wall.

It was of course on the cards that Miss Allison might not be on duty as a cashier, but I saw at once that she was. I saw this out of the corner of my eye as I went to the desk, just her nameplate at an open pigeon-hole and a glimpse of fair hair behind the glass screen. There was no one doing business with her. There was another customer further along the counter, talking to a male cashier. I made out a cheque for cash and put my credit card on top of it. Then I took a slip of paper and wrote, 'I need your help. About the graveyard.' I had thought the wording out in advance. I did not want to frighten her, but equally I did not want to risk a brush-off. I thought she was a girl who might or might not ask for help herself, but who would be ready to help if help was needed.

There was still nobody claiming her attention, and the other cashier was still busy with his customer along the counter. I went up to the pigeon-hole and pushed the cheque and credit card through, with the slip of paper on top of them. She must have seen me at the desk, because she was watching me as I came across to her. We exchanged conventional good-mornings, but she was watching me very carefully. Then she dropped her eyes and read what I had written on the slip of paper.

She did not bat an eye. For a moment she stayed quite still, looking down at the paper. Then she said, 'Yes,' in a brisk way, as if it was ordinary bank business. She left the cheque lying where it was, but picked up the card and the slip and retired to one side, where she busied herself with some sort of card index. I fancied it was routine procedure for checking that the credit card was not listed as missing or stolen. A moment or two later she was back with the card and another slip of paper in her hand. I could not see what she had done with my slip, but I felt sure it had been taken care of. She said, 'How would you like it?' and I told her singles, and she counted out the money and pushed it out to me with my credit card and her slip on top. I thanked her and folded the whole lot up round the card and stowed the bundle in an inside pocket. Then we said good morning to each other, and I walked out of the bank. I did not know what she had written on the slip, but there was certainly nothing wrong with the way she had managed it.

I walked back to my car, which was with a good many others in a public car park. There was a car pulled up on each side of it, but they were both empty. I unlocked the car and got into the driving seat and shut the door. Only then I pulled the folded bundle out of my inside pocket. I put the notes away with my others in my hip pocket and the credit card back in its usual place in my wallet. Then I looked at the slip. It said, 'The Yetts car park, six.' She wrote a very firm, clear hand, not distinguished in any way, but very workmanlike.

I knew where the Yetts were, though I had not been there. It was a local beauty spot on the outskirts of the town, where a burn came cascading down a hill-face between high rocky walls. There were picture postcards of it in all the shops, and the Council would have made a car park there for the sake of the summer visitors. There were probably litter baskets and benches to sit on over the water. I doubted if the locals went there now, except perhaps in the summer to empty the baskets and tidy up. Once a place like that has been surrendered to the visitors, no one loves it any more. At six o'clock on a winter evening it might as well be the North Pole. I wondered in fact if this was wise, but I assumed that Miss Allison knew what she was about, because she generally seemed to. It would make me a bit late home, even if we were not there long, but I had hardly expected her to manage anything earlier. Being by this time the complete James Bond, I took out my lighter and burnt the slip over the ashtray. I thought mine had probably gone to a watery death, but the car park did not provide the necessary facilities. Meanwhile I had the day to waste.

Aberennan at this time of the year had not much to offer the contemplative mind, and in any case I was not feeling contemplative. In fact I was feeling strung up and a bit nervous. The curious thing is that I was nervous simultaneously in two contradictory ways. I was nervous about the rather threatening thing I seemed to have got myself mixed up in, but at the same time I was still nervous of making a fool of myself. I knew I was not mistaken in thinking that the cottage had been searched, and I clung on to this fact with a sort of obstinate determination to make the worst of it. I wanted if possible to open the subject with Miss Allison, when we did meet, in such a way as would cover me to some extent in both directions, but my experience is that making up your mind in advance what you are going to say to a person is never much use. I did not think it was much good sitting in the car and thinking about it, but even if I got out of the car, I did not know what to do. I did not want to parade myself unnecessarily about Aberennan, certainly not on and off all day. It was a place I never as a rule spent more than an hour or two in. Finally I got back into the car and simply drove out of the town, but not on the road back to Kinlocheilean.

I got myself a meal of sorts at a pub on the road. The Scottish pub is still a long way behind the English pub, I suppose because the Scots take their drinking so seriously, but in the Highlands at least the remorseless pressures of the tripper trade are slowly taking effect. At least I should not be seriously hungry before I got home. Then I drove back into Aberennan, bought myself a paperback thriller and drove out again. There was a cinema, but at this time of the year there was only an evening show, which was no good to me. Before I drove out, I found my way to the Yetts, to make sure I knew how to get there, but I did not stop there.

At about twenty to six I drove back into the public car park. It was dark now. The car park was almost empty, and I put the car on the side furthest from the road. Then I got out, locked the car and started to walk. I had decided on this at some time in the afternoon. I thought two cars parked side by side in the Yetts car park, one with a noticeably southern number, would not be a good thing. A local car parked by itself in a place like that would be explained, if it was seen, in a way which had nothing to do with Miss Allison and me.

I walked into the Yetts only a minute or two before six. It was a dark place, because of the trees and rocks that overhung it, and very quiet except for the steady splashing of the water among the boulders. There was no car anywhere. I looked back along the road into the town, but could see no car approaching. I stood for a moment, suddenly disconcerted and apprehensive, and then a torch shone out of the darkness, floodlit me for a moment and then went out again. From somewhere behind it Miss Allison said, 'Good evening.'

I had whipped round, of course, when the torch came on, but now I was still dazzled by it and could see nothing. Then my eyes readjusted themselves to the darkness, and I saw her quite close to me, a small compact figure, swathed in a dark coat with something dark over her hair. I said, 'Good evening. You startled me.'

'I thought you'd come in the car,' she said.

'I thought you would,' I said. 'We're both too clever by half.' I had been right about her speech. She had something of the local intonations, but her pronunciation and use of words was standard English. I could not tell whether it was a deliberately acquired professional accomplishment, or whether she had perhaps been brought up or educated further south. I thought that with her friends she very likely spoke the local speech, but I was a stranger still and a southerner at that. At any rate, the effect was very charming.

She laughed, and that was pleasant to hear, too, and reassuring in that rather dreary place. 'Well, anyhow,' she said, 'let's get on with it now we are here. There's a seat over there. Shall we sit?'

I said, 'Lead on,' and followed her in the darkness till I saw the water foaming white ahead of us, and the straight back of a park bench dark against it. She sat down, and I sat down beside her. It was all very nocturnal and secret, but we spoke in normal voices because of the noise of the water.

She turned and looked at me. I could see her much more clearly now. It was less dark here, and my eyes were still improving. 'Well?' she said.

I said, 'We met at the graveyard. You were busy inside, but I don't know what you were doing. So far as I know, no one saw either of us that time. Quite soon after that

92

someone else, I don't know who, a man, went to the grave-yard to look for something but could not find it. I went there myself, out of curiosity, after I had seen you there, and someone saw me there. He told someone else, and the next day my house was entered and searched while I was away. I conclude that they suspect me of having taken whatever it was they wanted from the graveyard. I myself, naturally, suspect you, because I saw you there. Now. I don't know what all this is about, but I think there are dangerous people involved. So long as they have any reason to suspect me, I may be in some degree of danger myself—I don't know, but it seems possible. I don't know if they have any reason to suspect you. They don't know you went to the graveyard, and I'm certainly not telling any-one. But if they have other reasons for suspecting you, you may be in danger too. So I thought I'd better tell you the position. What I should like, of course, is for you to tell me what it's all about, so that I could know better how to deal with it. But that's up to you.'

She had turned away from me and was sitting staring in front of her with her hands clasped in her lap. She did not move for a bit even after I stopped talking. Then she shook her head, as if to herself, and turned to me. It was still only her head that moved. 'Oh dear,' she said, 'I'm sorry you've got involved.'

'That wasn't your fault,' I said. 'I needn't have gone back there. It was nothing you did.' She had turned her head away again. 'Look,' I said, 'I'm not imagining the whole thing, am I? It is something that might be danger-ous?'

'Oh yes,' she said, 'you're not imagining it. I suppose it could be dangerous. I don't know who these people are, but I imagine they could be dangerous.'

I said, 'I know, or I think I know, who some of them are, and believe me, they are.'

She said nothing for a bit. Then she turned to me again and said, 'All right. I'll tell you some of it. That's because I trust you. You won't tell anyone else, of course.'

I said, 'You've no reason to trust me.'

'I've no reason to distrust you,' she said. 'I know who you are, and I know you're not mixed up in it. And you liked me as soon as you saw me. I like people who do that.'

'That's uncommonly honest of you,' I said. 'It's true, of course. I liked you and admired you when we first met, and I still do. So far as my intentions go, you can trust me. I might be of more use to you if I knew more.'

She nodded. She was looking ahead of her again, staring out over the luminous, noisy water. She did not turn when she spoke, but I could hear her well enough. She said, 'I did take something from the graveyard. I knew it was there and where to look for it. I knew there'd be others looking for it later, or I thought there would be, and I decided to get it first. I thought I had a right to it. It was my brother who put it there.'

I said, 'Jimmy?' and she whipped round.

'How do you know?' she said.

'I don't. It was only a guess. I knew there'd been a Jimmy Allison working in Gleneilean before I went there, and I knew he came from Aberennan.'

She was staring at me, trying to see what she could of me in the strange phosphorescent darkness. She looked very uncompromising. 'Anything else?' she said.

I said, 'I heard he'd been in trouble later, after he left the glen. Just that. I don't know what sort of trouble.' I did not think it necessary to tell her that I had also heard that her brother was no damned good at all. Unless I was much mistaken in her, she probably knew that already.

She went on staring at me for a bit, and then nodded and turned away. I said, 'Where's Jimmy now?'

94

She said, 'In Canada.'

After that neither of us said anything for quite a long time. Then I said, 'Look—this thing, whatever it is—I don't know if you've still got it, but if you have, I think you'd better get rid of it.'

'I haven't,' she said. 'I know where it is. I could find it again. But I haven't got it.'

I said, 'Do these people know it was Jimmy who put it in the graveyard?'

'Oh yes. He told them. They knew he had it, originally, I mean, and he told them where he'd put it. That was quite recently. Just before he went to Canada. Only he'd told me first, and by the time he told them, I'd already moved it. But he didn't know that, not when he told them.'

'But don't you see,' I said, 'they must suspect you, if Jimmy's your brother. Are your parents alive?'

'No, there's just the two of us. But they've no reason to suppose Jimmy would have told me. He wouldn't have, normally. They'd have known that. He never told me anything if he could help it. It was only a very special chance he told me about this.'

I said, 'What's your name? I know it begins with M. What does M stand for?'

'Mary,' she said. 'Why?'

'No good reason. I just wanted to know.'

'Look,' she said, 'the position is this. No one can find this thing except me. They may suspect me. They may even suspect you. But they have nothing really to go on. Can we leave it at that for the moment? If anything fresh happens on my side, I promise I'll tell you. If anything happens on yours, you tell me. But unless anything does, let's leave it as it is.'

'If that's what you want,' I said. 'But I don't like it.'

She got up, a very quick, decisive movement, and I got up too. 'That's what I want,' she said. 'If the need arises, we can think again. But I still hope it won't.'

There was nothing more I could do. 'All right,' I said. 'But if the need arises, for God's sake be quick. I might or might not be able to help you, but I'd do my best.'

We were facing each other now. She looked very solemn and very young. 'Thank you,' she said. 'I'm glad it's you I have to trust and not someone else. Now I'm going to walk back into the town. Will you walk behind me, not too close, until we get into the streets? Then we each go our own way. All right?'

'All right,' I said. 'Off you go. Good-bye, Mary.'

She said, 'Good-bye, Mr Ainslie. And thank you again.' Then she turned and went, and after a little I went after her.

It was nearly half past eight when I got in, and I was hungry and depressed. And worried. I did not like it, I did not like any of it at all. I still liked Mary Allison, but that only made it worse.

CHAPTER TEN

Saturday was one of those days you get sometimes in the Highland winter when the weather seems to have moved in from the summer isles on the West Coast. There is a soft, hazy air, completely still, and a pale sunshine surprisingly warm on the skin. It is better than spring, because nothing is involved and you have nothing yet to hope for. You know it cannot last, and that is the beauty of it. It was a day when I wanted very much to be out on my own on the hill, and I hoped Macandrew would stand on his intention of not going. It was also in fact a day when I did not want very much to shoot anything, but I was committed now, and once I was out and taking Mr Sinclair's money, I should have to do my best. Still, if I was on my own, I could take my time, or perhaps get a single beast early in the day and let honour be satisfied with that.

When I drove into the Ardevie yard, the Landrover was standing in the middle facing eastwards, but I could not see Macandrew anywhere, and his rifle was not on the rack behind the driver's seat. It certainly looked as if he was not going out, but obviously I could not just take off on my own without seeing him. Also, to be safe I needed another box of cartridges. I parked my car in the usual place and walked across and put my rifle in the Landrover.

Then I waited in the quiet early brightness, not quite sure what to do. If I had known where Macandrew had his quarters, I could have tried for him there, but I did not, and in any case I thought he would be out and about somewhere.

I had not been there more than a minute when he came out of the back door of the lodge with a box of cartridges in his hand. 'You'll be needing these,' he said. I might have known he would think of it. You never go out on the hill without plenty of ammunition. It is better to bring back a lot of unused cartridges than to find yourself with a wounded beast and nothing to kill it with. I had been shooting well enough up to now with that beautiful little rifle, but then I had had the inestimable advantage of Macandrew's stalking. I had been taken up to a safe firing position, and the only decision I had had to make was which beast to shoot at. Today it would be very different, and my quality as a stalker might test my quality as a shot.

'You're not coming out?' I said.

He shook his head. 'I'll no come the day,' he said. 'There's things I must look to here. Let's see what you can do on your own.'

'Where'd I better try?' I said.

He turned and looked out eastward along the face of the hill, his brow wrinkled with concentration. You could not possibly see anything from there. It was almost as if he was trying the wind. In fact I think he was seeing the whole picture in his mind, the hill, the weather, the wind and what the deer would be making of it all. Then he jerked his head slightly and turned to me. 'You'd best try Meall Ruadh,' he said. 'If they're no there, they'll be away up on the high tops. It will no be all that easy, maybe. But go and have a look.'

'I will,' I said. My earlier nonchalance had vanished already. I was determined now to get something. I dropped the box of cartridges into my pocket and climbed into the driving seat. The window was open, and he was standing just outside. I said, 'I know what I wanted to ask you. That Jimmy Allison you mentioned—was he the one that worked for Davie Bain?'

He looked at me very straight, as if he was wondering why I had asked. My question had been a disingenuous one, of course—I had no reason to suppose that Jimmy had ever worked for Davie—and a man like Macandrew could smell a touch of disingenuity as I had felt for a moment he could smell the deer. 'He never worked for yon Davie,' he said. 'Not as you might say officially. What he may have done for him between whiles I wouldna ken. He was in his pocket, all right.'

I had got what I wanted, and was anxious to re-establish my innocence. 'But he never worked in the garage?' I said.

'No there,' he said, 'never. First for yon Colonel Thompson and then for Mr Sinclair. Then he was away off back to Aberennan.'

I nodded and started the engine. 'I must have been thinking of someone else,' I said. He did not say anything. He just went on looking at me. I let in the clutch and moved off eastward along the track. I did not look back.

Jimmy was Mary's brother, but he was no damned good and had been in Davie Bain's pocket, whatever that meant. Then at some time he had hidden something in the grave-yard of the Maceacherns. It was something Davie Bain wanted very badly, but Jimmy had not, apparently, told him where it was. Then at some point he had told Mary, and she had taken the thing and put it somewhere else. Then Jimmy had told Davie, and he had gone to look for it and found it no longer there. But the time-scale of the whole story was completely obscure. I did not know at what intervals the various things had happened, or what had happened during the intervals. Above all, I did not know how long the thing had been in the graveyard. If it was a long time, I could not understand why Davie, who had Jimmy in his pocket, had not been told it was there until in fact it no longer was. And I remembered now what Mary had said. She had said that Davie (only she did not know it was Davie) had known that Jimmy had had the thing originally. This made it more difficult to understand than ever. For all Mary's sturdiness, I saw Jimmy as a petty crook, the sort of man who would take anyone's teeth if you no watched him, and a man who, if he had any dealings with the formidable Davie, would be almost completely at his mercy. That was what Macandrew would have meant when he said he was in his pocket. And yet he had managed not to tell him, I did not know for how long, but long enough, something he had badly wanted to know. It did not make sense, not on the facts I had. But then Mary had not told me the whole story. In any case, there was nothing I could do unless something fresh happened. The trouble was that if it did happen, I did not think it would happen to me. I thought it would happen to Mary, and Mary on her own was no match for Davie.

I found myself bumping along the track much too fast, and this would not do. For one thing, now that I was in the driver's seat, I should be keeping an eye out for the beasts up on the face, and on this going any sort of divided attention meant driving very slowly indeed. For another, if the beasts were there, it might worry them, and that was the last thing I wanted. A vehicle that crawled and did not stop they did not mind. One that went bouncing noisily along the track might put them on their guard from the start, and that would make the stalking much more difficult. I pulled back to a steady ten miles an hour, and began to keep an eye on the hill-face. I did not expect to see anything before I reached the Meall, if then, but with the deer you never know.

In fact I came under the north face of Meall Ruadh without seeing anything. There I stopped the car. There was nothing else to do. Wherever I stopped it, it could be seen from somewhere on the hill, and I did not know where the beasts were or indeed if there were any on the face at all. I eased myself round the gear lever and got out on the nearside, with the car between me and the hill. Then I put my head round the side of the windscreen and looked long and hard all over the face. There was nothing wrong with my long sight, and I knew what the deer looked like at a distance. This is important, because the in-experienced eye, and even the experienced eye that is out of practice, simply cannot see the beasts on the hill at any sort of a distance, even when in fact they are there to be seen. You have got to know what to look for. I looked for it very hard, but I could still see nothing.

I wet my finger in my mouth and held it up, Boy Scout fashion, to try the wind. To ordinary observation there was no wind at all, but the air on the hill is never quite still, and whatever movement there is you must allow for as much as a palpable breeze. I felt nothing at first, and then the faintest chill on the southern side of my uplifted finger. Whatever air there was was moving off the hill. That was something at least. There was nothing for it now but to walk up the face, taking the ground as I came to it, and hoping that there might be beasts there, and that I might see them before they saw me. I took the rifle out and loaded it. Then I went round the car and began my long slow walk up the hill.

Now that I was out of the car and on my own in the still weather, a touch of my earlier mood returned. I still meant to get a beast if I could, but I no longer minded very much whether I did or not. I did the right things automatically, watching the hill ahead all the time, making sure that the wind was still coming to meet me and clearing each new piece of ground as I opened it up before I moved into it. But the tension was not there, and my senses were not really at full stretch. The hunting instinct is a phrase much bandied about in all sorts of figurative senses and unsuitable contexts, but when you are on the hill with a rifle, it represents a very real experience. What your non-shooting man finds it difficult to understand is that it is not essentially different, as an experience, from what you feel if you have only a camera or a pair of birdwatcher's glasses. There is the same association between your mind and that of the beasts, the same attempt to bridge the gap between you. It becomes a sympathy, even a conscious affection, because it is very difficult to observe any living creature, human or otherwise, in secret and from a distance, without developing this sort of sympathy. There is nothing hypocritical in this, whatever your practical intentions, because you are not pretending to anyone. There is no third party there to pretend to. In any case, I could never see why the charge of hypocrisy should be confined to the shooting man. It is not only vegetarians who like to watch the lambs playing.

It is only when your mind and those of the creatures observed actually meet and clash that your egotism may re-assert itself. In the case of the deer, it is when they have out-sensed and out-witted you, and you are left, for all your patience and exertion, with an empty hill and an unfired rifle. Then you may feel, at least for a time, a bloody-minded determination to get even with them, to establish your human superiority in conditions in which your human capabilities are on balance at a disadvantage. Even so, there is no hatred or anger in it, only an exasperation with your own human short-comings. That Saturday morning, as I worked my way up the face of Meall Ruadh in the soft sunlight, I had hardly reached even the initial stage of the experience. The deer were not there to observe. I went on, doing my best in a fairly detached sort of way, seeking the experience but not yet having it.

When I was about half-way up the face, I stopped and sat down, looking northwards across the width of Gleneilean. This was a luxury I could not enjoy when I was out with Macandrew. Macandrew sat down only to rest, between one lot of work and another, as heaven knows at his age he was entitled to do. I had done no real work yet, and I was not tired. I stopped and sat down only because I did not want to go on doing what I was doing. I wanted to look at something other than the hill-face immediately ahead of me. In a sense I was resting, because even if the elaborate care I was exercising was to a large extent automatic and instinctive, it was still elaborate. It made demands on the nervous system rather than the mind, and when the nervous system gets tired, it cannot be beaten along as the mind can. It simply gets less efficient. Even if I did not feel tired, the chances were that I was being less careful. But that was not really what I had in mind. I sat down merely to enjoy the day and the view.

The forestry trees were well below me here. I could not see the near shore of the loch, because of that last steep plunge of the face down to the water, but I could see the water on the far side, and I saw the trees as a thin, dark fringe outlined against it. Beyond the water, the north side of the glen went up, ridge beyond ridge, crest beyond crest, in interlocking lines of colour, till the brown faded into gold, and the gold into pearl, and the pearl into the palest blue, and above the blue, floating as detached as a cloud, the snow on Ben Strohan gleamed in the sun. In all that vast landscape I could see nothing, except the forestry trees, which man had had any hand in; and the trees might still have been there if man had not existed.

But I knew man was there all right, busy with his own affairs, angry with other men because they interfered with them, and for the most part as oblivious of the landscape as the landscape seemed of him. And the trouble was that, for all my physical detachment, I knew that my own mental detachment was lost. It was lost because that one morning I had yielded to my curiosity and stopped to look at someone's head and shoulders moving purposefully about in the graveyard of the Maceacherns. I could not see the graveyard from here. It was down under the trees, thrust out into that placid, unseen water. But for me, now, it disturbed the whole landscape.

I thought it was time I went on. On the instant caution re-asserted itself, and before I stood up, I turned my head and looked at the hill-face above me. And it was at that moment, while I was still sitting with the rifle beside me, that I suddenly saw the beasts. I could just see them, from the level my head was now on, over the top of a rounded fold of the hill. They could have seen the top of my head if they had looked. If I stood up, they could have seen most of me. They were not very far away. How long they had been there I had no idea. I had not been sitting very long, but whether they had been there when I sat down, or whether they had moved there since, I could not tell. It was possible that in that last wavering of attention, when I had made up my mind to sit down and was looking for somewhere to sit, I had in fact moved up within sight of them, but had not seen them, nor they me. At any rate, there they were.

I rolled sideways off the stone I was sitting on and lay there for a moment, feeling for my cap and my rifle. I had taken my cap off when I sat down, but luckily the back of my head had been towards the beasts. Now that I had to face them, I needed the cap, and pulled well down. The upper part of the human face, the forehead and cheeks, is extraordinarily visible on the hill, especially as a moving object. The smooth, hairless skin throws back the light at almost any angle, and looks like nothing else in nature. That is why for stalking you wear a drab cloth cap with a peak you can just see under. The sort of cap that covers only the hair, a beret for example, leaves you at a disadvantage, because in the nature of things you have to keep your face up to see ahead, especially if you are working up-hill. I put my cap on and settled it firmly on my head. I cocked the rifle, as quietly as I could, and put the safety-catch over. Then I got on to my knees and began to go forward.

When I had gone a little way, I got my feet under me and stood up, very slowly, crouching. I had moved in under the concave face of the fold, and I was standing almost straight before I saw the beasts again. Then I crouched and went on forward, bent low with my rifle held cross-wise at the level of my knees. When you are moving up on the beasts under a fold of the ground, you do not move at a level which will bring your head at some point within sight of them, because it is very difficult to control your forward movement with enough delicacy, and your head may come up much too suddenly. Instead you make your forward movement at a level and for a distance which you know leaves you totally invisible, and then, very slowly, raise your head and take a fresh sighting. I went another fifteen yards crouching. Moving on your feet is always much quicker than any sort of crawling, but a crouched walk is very bad for the breath, and if you reach your firing point badly out of breath, it makes accurate shooting difficult. This time when I stopped and began to straighten up, I saw the beasts almost at once. I dropped and went forward on hands and knees. I was getting near the top of the fold now, and after my next sighting it was belly-work or nothing. I made for a heather clump that would give my head and shoulders cover while I got my rifle up, and when I got up to it, there they were.

It was only a small herd, perhaps fifteen beasts, but they were grazing quietly enough. All the same, you cannot trust a wind as light as that, because the slightest back-eddy of air along the hill-face will betray you. For a second or two I let my breathing settle, though my heart was bumping as it always does when you come to the point. Then I came up into the aim. I had picked my beast already. There was a group of three in the middle of the line of beasts, a big hind, a medium-sized beast and a small calf. I knew what that meant. It meant that the last-year's calf was still running with the hind, as they do until they get collected into a stag's herd. She was a grown, shootable beast, and she would be breeding herself next year, but for the moment she had nothing dependent on her. It is a beast I always pick if I can.

I waited until she was stock-still and then fired a very careful shot. I did not think there could be anything wrong with it, but I worked the bolt the moment I had fired, as you always do in case a second shot is needed. All their heads came up when I fired, and of course they saw me at once. Just for a moment they stared at me, all eyes and ears, and then the big hind snorted and was off, with the new calf after her. My beast went a few yards and then stopped. I knew then that it was all right, but I had my sights on her in case. She did not look at me. She just stood there for a moment uncertainly, and then she went down slowly and rolled over flat. One leg kicked twice as she lay, but I knew she was already dead. It was only a matter of seconds since I had fired, but the rest of the herd was nowhere in sight. They had vanished, in the way they do, literally into the ground, but I was no longer interested in them. I had got my beast with a clean shot, and that would do for the day. My tension collapsed in the usual enormous relief. I stood up, unloaded the rifle and walked forward to do what I had to do.

It was not a bad drag. The beast was not a big one, and I was not too far up the face. It was going to be an easy day. I did not altogether deserve this, because the truth was that the beasts had found me and not I them, but I was not going to tell Macandrew that. He had sent me off doubtfully, to do the best I could in difficult conditions, and I should get in earlier than he expected, and with a well shot beast. I went on with the job placidly.

It was still full daylight when I left the lodge and started for home, and I had hardly turned out on to the main road when I met Davie Bain driving westwards. As always on that road, we had to slow down and pass each other carefully. He recognised me at once, but looked neither disconcerted nor hostile. As we crawled past each other, his great face split into a wide, jovial smile, and his hand came up to the peak of his deer-stalker. I smiled and saluted in return. I did not warm to the sight of him, but I felt no differently towards him from the way I had always felt. At least he was here and not making trouble in Aberennan. Not for the first time, I wondered suddenly whether I was not, so far as my part in it was concerned, imagining the whole damned thing.

CHAPTER ELEVEN

It would have been pleasant if the golden weather had held over the Sunday, but of course it did not. You cannot really expect more than a day of it at that time of the year, and I suppose it is in fact no more than a temporary phase in a changing pattern of weather. On Sunday the rain came in from the west, with a steady breeze behind it. It was still not particularly cold, but very wet indeed. The snow was already gone from everywhere but the high tops, and the rain and wind got rid of a lot more of it even there. The whole landscape, which yesterday had been pale gold, turned almost black under a dark sky, and it looked as if it might be very unpleasant on the hill next day. Apart from extremes of cold, wet is the great bugbear. The whole country is little more than a thin skin of peaty soil over solid rock, and when it is saturated, it is like working on a wet sponge. If it is raining and blowing at the same time, the wet gets at you from every direction. You cannot wear waterproofs, in the ordinary sense, because they are cumbersome and noisy to move in, and once they are wet they reflect a lot of light. You have to rely on your tweeds to throw most of the water off, and wear enough under them to maintain a dry layer between them and your skin.

However, for the moment there was no need to go out

in it, and I certainly did not need exercise. It is only the man doing hard physical work during the week who can fully relish the total physical relaxation which Sunday affords. I got up in a leisurely way and put on clean clothes, and spent the day doing small chores about the house. This included a good deal of darning. The long stockings you wear on the hill are still mostly wool, and lack the almost uncanny resistance to wear which the artificial fibres have. You are lucky if you get through a day without springing a hole somewhere, and unless you keep up with your darning, you soon find yourself with nothing to wear. But there are worse occupations than darning before a wood fire while the rain falls outside. The day passed pleasantly enough, and I did not find it in me to worry much about anything. I was still to some extent under the influence of my casual meeting with Davie Bain the evening before. There was no great logic in this, but if you have been building a man up into a bogeyman in your mind, and then suddenly meet him face to face without his doing anything threatening or suspicious, there is an inevitable slackening in your feelings towards him. So during almost the whole of that Sunday Davie Bain did nothing to disturb my peace of mind. I was wrong, in fact, but at least I got the benefit of my mistake.

It got dark very early, and I drew all the curtains to shut out the last of a day which had little to make me want to keep it. The burn was in spate, and I could hear it tumbling down among its rocks. What with that and the noise of the wind and rain on the house, there was a steady background of sound outside, so that the light and quietness inside seemed very isolated from an uncomfortable if not particularly hostile world. I suppose that was why I did not hear the car come up the track. I heard nothing until there was a sharp knocking on the door. It did not sound desperate, but it was very firm and persistent. I could think of no one who would be out on such a night but Black Harry and Jock, and the knocking did not sound at all like Black Harry. Not that I gave myself much time to speculate. I went to the door in a state of suspended surprise, switching on the porch light as I went. It was Mary Allison.

She looked very small in the light from the door. She was not at all wet, and I could see a car standing behind her. It had no lights on. She said, 'Can the car be seen from the road?'

'Not when the lights are off,' I said.

She nodded. 'May I come in?' she said. I stepped back and let her in and shut and locked the door behind her.

I pointed to the sitting room door. 'In there,' I said. She went in, and I switched out the porch light and followed her.

She stood for a moment looking round the room. 'It's nice,' she said. 'You make yourself very comfortable.' I was pleased at that. All the same, I was for some reason glad that she had not found me darning stockings. She took off her coat and put it over the back of a chair. She was wearing something dark and plain. I did not take much notice of it.

'Sit down,' I said. 'Can I get you anything?'

She thought for a moment. I think she really did not quite know whether she wanted anything, and was not going to answer either way on purely social grounds. 'No,' she said, 'I don't think so, thank you. I mustn't stop longer than I can help. Am I keeping you from your supper?'

'Not yet,' I said. She was sitting on the sofa now, with one hand held out to the fire. She looked very nice. I sat in my chair on the other side of the fireplace. 'Tell me, then,' I said. 'I take it something has happened? I'm glad you're all right, anyhow.'

She nodded. 'I've had my burglary,' she said.

'When?'

'Yesterday afternoon.'

'You were out, I take it?'

'I was out walking, yes. It was a lovely day, and I do a lot of walking at the week-ends. I mean—real walking, you know? On the hills.'

'Good,' I said. I had thought that springy way she moved argued a body in good condition. 'And when you got back, you found it? Was there much to see?'

'Much to see?' she said. 'The place was a shambles. It was a bit horrifying, in fact. All right, they'd searched the place, I suppose. But they'd been pretty vicious about it. I mean, you don't have to smash a teapot to see what's inside it. I think—I think I was meant to be frightened. I was.'

'I'm sorry,' I said. 'What did you do?'

'Phoned the police, of course. What else could I do? They came and were very good. I don't know what they made of it. There wasn't much missing, in fact.'

'There were things missing?'

'Yes, but I think that was just for appearances. A transistor radio. The only decent bit of jewellery I had. I'm insured, of course. It's not that I mind about.'

'What did you tell the police?'

'Nothing, I'm afraid. I wanted to talk to you first. I just let them draw their own conclusions. I spent the day tidying up and making out my insurance claim. Then as soon as it was dark I came along here.'

I nodded. 'So far, so good,' I said. 'Now, are you going to tell me the rest of the story, or am I going to ask you questions?'

'I'll tell you. But ask questions as I go along if you want to.'

'Right,' I said. 'Off you go, then.'

She had got both hands clasped on her knees now, and

was staring into the fire. It was exactly as she had sat on the bench at the Yetts. She said, 'Jimmy's my younger brother. He's three years younger than I am, and I've looked after him, more or less, since my mother died. I'm very fond of Jimmy, but I don't honestly think he's much good.' I thought that was the final nail in Jimmy's coffin, but I did not say anything. 'He had various jobs after he left school, but he never really settled to anything. I'm afraid he's one of those people who feel the world owes them a living, and he doesn't see why he should work for it. I carried him quite a lot, in fact. Well, I don't mind that. The flat was ours, and my pay's quite good. But of course I was worried about him. I mean, I expect I'll get married some time, and I wasn't taking Jimmy with me. Not that there was anything serious to worry about at first. Just this general incapacity of making a go of anything or facing up to anything. Then he got a job out here. You know about that. I was pleased about it, because I thought he'd have real work to do and be out of mischief. I couldn't have been more wrong. I don't know what it was, but it was while he was out here that the trouble really started. He wasn't here long, not more than six months or so, and when he came back, I pretty well knew he was getting into real trouble. He never told me anything. He never had much, and what he did say wasn't always very reliable. But he was out a lot, especially at night, and used to get telephone calls he didn't explain. And he had money. Not all the time, but every now and then, and sometimes quite a lot of it. I knew it couldn't be honestly come by, but I couldn't get anything out of him, and if I tried to ask him, he turned a bit nasty.'

Her voice trailed away, and for a moment she looked thoroughly woe-begone. Then she recovered herself and turned to me and smiled. 'Oh well,' she said, 'why elaborate? It's the usual story, I suppose. Why our boys leave home, or officer, what have I done wrong, he used to be a good boy. And it ended the usual way. The police came. He'd been caught with a stolen car, and nobody believed his explanation, and small blame to them. I don't think he'd stolen it, mind you. I think he'd just been told off to get it away. Anyway, he kept his mouth shut. Honour among thieves, if you like, but being Jimmy I'd say it was a mixture of fright and calculation. The court knew he was only the mug, of course. They fined him a couple of hundred quid and told him to go straight or else, and the fine was paid and he didn't go straight.

'Well, that's the background. Now we get to the part that matters. I won't tell you my side of it—I mean, how I saw it at the time. That's not the point. I'll tell you what I'm pretty certain happened. It took me some time to put together. Whoever was running him told him off to do a breaking and entering job, and told him what to look for, and promised him a big cut on delivery of the goods. They must have trusted him more than I would have, but I suppose he'd proved himself reliable once, and they took a chance on him. Anyway, he made a fair boorach of it.'

It was the first time she had dropped into the vernacular. 'A what?' I said.

She smiled. 'A proper mix-up,' she said, and went back to English. 'The owner caught him at it, and he hit him and bolted. Mercifully, being Jimmy, he didn't hit him very hard. But in all the excitement he left marks all over the place, and of course by now he had a record, and the police were on to him at once. The owner told the police there was cash missing, but I don't believe that myself. He was a bit of a doubtful character himself. He ran the local betting-shop, but that was his more respectable side. In fact, Jimmy got what he was sent to get, and set off hell for leather to deliver it to whoever it was that wanted it. At least, I think he must have. Anyway, he headed this

113

way. What happened then I don't know. Either he couldn't find his man, or he thought the police were after him, and panicked. Anyway, he hid the loot. You don't need to be told where. Then he headed back to Aberennan, and was picked up almost as soon as he got there. This time he got eighteen months. There was the violence, you see. He still didn't talk. I know why, this time. He thought he had a fortune stashed away, and could pick it up when he came out. Meanwhile he was safe in jail and no one could get at him. He changed his mind later. He was never a very brave one, Jimmy, and he was scared of the boss all right. But by then I'd put my oar in.' She took her eyes off the fire and looked at me. 'Any questions?' she said.

I said, 'Finish the story first. We left Jimmy in jail. Now you say he's in Canada. How and since when?'

'That was my doing,' she said. 'I had to think of something for him. For when he came out, I mean. Otherwise he'd have been in and out the rest of his life. So I wrote to Uncle Bob in Canada. He's Dad's brother. Dad died when Jimmy was only a kid. That was his trouble, really, I think. Mum was no good with him at all. She couldn't see through him as Dad would have. I could, but if I said anything, I only got shouted at. I'd never seen Uncle Bob, or not to remember, but I reckoned if he was anything like Dad, he might handle Jimmy. And he farms way out. Man's life and all that. So I wrote and told him what had happened, and asked him if he'd take on Jimmy and try to knock some sense into him. He said he would and he has. I bet Jimmy's hardly got his breath back yet. But at least he's away from here.'

'What about the loot?' I said.

'Yes, sorry—I've got out of step a bit. That came first, of course.'

'My fault,' I said. 'I shouldn't have asked questions.'

'Well—I used to go and see Jimmy, of course, when I

could. He didn't take kindly to jail. He was only a kid, mentally, I mean. What he needed was standing hard on his own feet, and of course jail doesn't do that for you. I tried to sell him Uncle Bob. He more or less agreed, but I think what he really had in mind was to collect his loot and go and make a bit of hay in Canada, only not Uncle Bob's hay. Then he got ill. Really ill. I mean, they sent for me pretty sharp to go and see him in the jail hospital. Pneumonia. He never had much of a chest, and I don't suppose the life helped. I went, of course. He had a temperature of God knows what and was all away. I think he thought he was dying. I think he wanted to, just to show them. I didn't think he was, nor did they, but he put on a death-bed scene for my benefit. Well, perhaps that's not quite fair. He didn't really know what he was about.'

I said, 'You're a tough girl, aren't you, Mary? Do you mind if I call you Mary?'

'No,' she said. 'You'd be tough if you'd had Jimmy all those years.'

'All right. Sorry. Go on.'

'Well, he told me about the loot, do you see? Where he'd put it. I was to have it if anything happened to him. All that. As if it was his life's savings. I said I would, of course, but I didn't think it would come to that. And it didn't. I mean, not like that. He got over it, of course. I wasn't quite sure, afterwards, whether he remembered telling me about the loot. But I wondered about it. Anyway, he got his full remission, what with his health and all that. I think they were anxious to get rid of him. As soon as I had a date for his release I got the Canadian thing all laid on. Air passage, flight, everything. He had a passport, thank God. I shouldn't have liked trying to get him one. And he was only visiting relations, not emigrating. I wasn't going to give him time to change his mind, you see. I was going to pick him up at the jail gate and pretty well drive him straight to Renfrew and put him on his plane. I knew they'd be after him the moment he came out because of the loot. They knew he'd had it, you see, but they didn't know where it was. That was when I began to think about it seriously. I thought if he got his hands on it, one of two things would happen. Either he'd play safe and hand it over, in which case they'd pay him his cut and before I knew it, he'd be back in business again. Or he'd try to get away with it, in which case I didn't know what they'd do to him. I couldn't see them letting him do that, not whatever plans I made. So I decided to play safe. I went and found it and put it somewhere else.'

'How?' I said.

'How what?'

'How did you get there and back? I didn't see any car.'

'Oh that. I walked.'

'Where from, in God's name?'

'From near Kinlocheilean. I left my car in a field and came in along the tops. I did it easily in the day.'

'All right,' I said. 'Sorry I interrupted.'

'Well—he came out a couple of days later, and I collected him and took him home. I was going to drive him to Renfrew that evening. But they knew, of course. They were probably waiting for him too, only I didn't give them a chance to get at him. But he hadn't been home half an hour when they phoned. I let him talk to them. Well, I couldn't stop him. When he'd finished, I cornered him. He tried to brush me off, of course, but I had him cold. I said if he'd told them where the stuff was, he'd better think again, because it was no longer there. Then he really broke up. Poor Jimmy. He had told them, of course. He was scared stiff of them, and now he was more scared than ever. He raved at me, but I was ready for that.

116

I said didn't he think in the circumstances we'd better get moving, and he was ready right enough. So while they were racing out to the graveyard, I was racing Jimmy to Renfrew. I put him on the plane and watched it take off. I know he got there. I had a cable from Uncle Bob.' She smiled suddenly. 'It said "Consignment received in poor condition, but will do my best." I'd like to meet Uncle Bob some time. It was late when I got back, but they must have been waiting. As soon as I was in, the phone went. It was a man asking for Jimmy. I told him he'd gone abroad and wouldn't be back. He just rang off. I didn't see what they could do. Then I found you'd got involved, and here we are.'

I said, 'I knew you were a cool one as soon as I saw you. By God, I was right, too.'

'I'm not so cool now,' she said. 'Not after yesterday. What do we do?'

'Where is the loot?' I said.

'Up on the hill. Straight up from the graveyard, just above the forestry. I can find it any time. No one else can.' She looked at me very straight.

'What does it consist of, then?'

'I don't know.'

'But you handled it.'

'A box,' she said. 'Not very big. A metal box with a bit of plastic sheet wrapped round it. I don't know what's inside.'

'Whatever it is,' I said, 'hand it over, Mary.'

'Who to?'

'The police.'

'What, and have it go back to Mr McNair of the betting shop? You don't know Mr McNair. It probably wasn't his to start with. And Jimmy did a year in jail for it. Not till I know what's inside it.'

'You're playing a dangerous game, Mary.'

She got up, quickly, as she did everything. 'Look,' she said. 'They can't know I've got it. They may think Jimmy took it with him.'

'He didn't have time to get it,' I said. 'They know that.'

'They can't even know it was ever in the graveyard. He could have been leading them up the garden path.'

'I doubt if they think that. They probably know their Jimmy. You didn't hear what he said to them on the phone.'

She said, 'I must go. If they know I'm here, we're really in trouble.' She put her coat on before I could give her a hand with it. 'Will you help me?' she said.

'Do what?'

'Collect the box and see what's inside. I haven't quite got the nerve to go alone.'

I said, 'Well, thank God for that. From what you say, it's on Ardevie ground, and as it happens, I've got a right to go there. Of a sort, anyway. All right. When?'

'Next week-end. I can't get away before.'

'All right. Now you go. Drive straight along the south shore and out on to the main road. I'll be a few minutes behind you. As far as the main road, anyhow. Just in case.'

'I'd be glad of that,' she said. 'Do you mind?'

'I'm coming whatever you say.'

'Thank you,' she said. She went into the porch and I went after her. She turned and said again, 'I'm glad it's you.'

'So am I,' I said, but I was not at all sure it was true.

We went out and locked the house behind us. She backed her car without fuss and went off down the track. I ran to the garage and went after her. I saw her tail-lights once or twice at bends of the road, but there was nothing else anywhere. There never is on a Sunday night. When she turned out on to the main road beyond Kinlocheilean, I stopped and came home. I had not had my supper yet, and tomorrow I must be up on the hill after the hinds again. But at least it had stopped raining.

CHAPTER TWELVE

The next week was a very hard one indeed. I suppose Macandrew had in fact been letting me in lightly, and now he was getting down to business. During our first week we had each put in four days on the hill—Macandrew had been out on the Friday, when I was at Aberennan, and had got two beasts—and we had had a total of twelve for the short week. An average of one and a half beasts a rifle a day was not bad, and it still made good economic sense from Mr Sinclair's point of view. At present prices a well grown hind could be worth forty pounds in the larder, and whatever he was proposing to pay me for my work, it would certainly not be sixty pounds a day. But at that rate it would take us some time to get in our quota, and Macandrew, like all good keepers, was out to protect his laird's interests so long as they did not conflict too sharply with his own. So now the pressure was on, and Macandrew himself, in his deliberate, calculated way, was inexhaustible. There was no question now, if we got some beasts in the first few hours, of getting them back in and making an early day of it. We would get the beasts into the Landrover and the tailboard up on them, and then he would push his cap back on his head and pass a hand over his bald crown, looking at me in his mild, quizzical way. 'We'd maybe better just take a look ayont Corrie Lomach,' he would say, or wherever the ground was which he thought the beasts might be favouring in these conditions, and which we had not been on in the past forty-eight hours or so. That was always the phrase, and I knew by now what it meant. It meant another drive along the track, and another long steady walk up the hill, and if we were lucky another long stalk and another equally long drag back to the track. I say 'lucky', and I still on the whole meant that, because I was still fully committed to the job and almost desperately anxious to have good results to show Mr Sinclair. There were of course times when I found myself in my weakness hoping that the beasts would not be there, but if they were, I did everything in my power to make sure we got some.

The weather did not help. It was wet and windy and still relatively mild, which meant that the beasts tended to be far up, and we got very wet from the outside getting up to them and wet with sweat getting them down. We got wet and dried out several times in the day, and once my body had got used to it, it did me no harm at all. Macandrew himself, like all his sort, seemed impervious to the weather, and I soon learned to be the same. I had a warm house to get back to, and my clothes were always dry before I put them on again next day. The days were getting shorter all the time, and it was always lights on in the larder now when we got back and full darkness before I got home. I enjoyed it, not out of masochism, but because I was doing a hard job well, and thereby earning the respect of two men whom I myself greatly respected. To a man at least I do not know any surer guarantee of satisfaction. I do not know about women. I think they are less ready to accept another person's scale of values.

It was on the Tuesday that I started having trouble with my car. It was increasingly difficult to start, both in the mornings when I left home and in the evenings when I left Ardevie. I was fairly certain it was the ignition, and the fact that the car had to stand out in the wet all day in the lodge yard did not help. It was upsetting in two ways. For one, the last thing I wanted when I got home in the evening was an exploratory session with the car in the garage. Exploratory it would have to be, because I am not much of a mechanic, and beyond trying the few obvious things I seldom know where to look for the answer when a car does not work as it should, especially if the fault is an electrical one. The other thing irked me much more. If the car was going wrong, the only place I could look for help was Davie Bain's garage in Kinlocheilean, and at that particular time I had the profoundest wish not to have any sort of dealings with Davie at all. The result was that I worried about the thing, but did nothing very decisive about it. I did make the effort to have the plugs out one evening and check them, but I could find nothing wrong with them. I thought this probably meant the coil, and in my experience coils are things which, when they do go wrong, simply have to be replaced. If the car lasted the week, I could of course drive it out at the week-end to some garage beyond Kinlocheilean, and get the job done there. But for one thing I did not think it would, and for another I had promised to meet Mary at the week-end, though I did not yet know when or where. But the truth is that I was not in a state to do any very constructive thinking at all. All day, and indeed well beyond the short hours of daylight, I drove myself to my physical limits in pursuit of the Ardevie quota of hinds, and every night I wondered whether the car would start in the morning, but was too tired to make up my mind what I should do if it did not.

On the Friday morning it would not start of itself at all, but I manhandled it out of the garage and ran it ruth- lessly down the jolting track to the road, with the gears in third and my foot down on the clutch. Just before I got to the tarmac I let the clutch in, and just before the car lost all its way the engine fired and kept on firing. I drove on to Ardevie, but I knew that, on the level yard of the lodge and after it had been standing all day in the damp, I had next to no hope of getting it moving again in the evening. I told Macandrew, and he said, 'Och, we'll phone yon Davie, and he'll send one of his boys over. If he no comes, I'll drive you back.' But he was in a hurry, because my trouble with the car had made me late, and the early hours of daylight are of especial value in the shooting of the hinds. The beasts come down in the night and move up again at sunrise, and the longer you leave them, the further you have to go for them. He bundled me into the Landrover and I knew he had not phoned when we left, but in view of his promise to see me home, I could not argue with him. In any case, you did not argue with Macandrew, or not in anything that concerned the hinds. And in one way at least he had settled my mind for me. It had to be Davie Bain now, and I supposed Macandrew was right in saying that it would be only one of the hands we should see at Ardevie. As usual, I had been making a bugbear of the man, but that was the effect he had on me. Also I thought the car would be all right now for the week-end, and that was one thing less to worry about. Like all poor mechanics, I had an implicit faith in the ministrations of the expert.

The weather was better now, colder but drier, but we had a bad day with the beasts, and I burdened myself from the start with a sense of guilt because I had made us late getting out. The wind had gone more into the north, which on that ground made the whole manoeuvre much more laborious. We drove past the Meall Ruadh without seeing any beasts, but Macandrew stopped the car, and we made our way in southward along the low ground, as we had that first day, and then turned and walked up the eastern face of the hill, with the wind blowing fairly well across us. As always when I was with Macandrew, I left the walk up entirely to him, walking a few yards behind him, stopping when he stopped and moving on again when he moved. There was in fact nothing more for me to do. So long as it stays together, any stalking party moves in line ahead, as indeed, when they are really on the move, the deer do themselves, and I suppose for more or less the same reasons. Provided you are moving steadily enough, the unexpected, which to the deer means danger and to the stalker means the deer, must always lie ahead, and your best chance of seeing it before it sees you is to present no more than a single body for its observation. Only the leading body must be the one best able to cope with the unexpected when it occurs, and the others, having surrendered their independent judgement, have nothing to do but follow, and observe, their leader. When a hind and calf run, the calf falls in on the hind's heels, and if there is a second-year calf running with them, it takes middle place in the line. The tendency of human children to get ahead, mentally and even physically, of their parents is the privilege of a dominant species, and even so may not always be the best way of moving.

Nevertheless, on this occasion the thing went wrong, because I saw the beasts before Macandrew did. We had just made our regular pause on the crest of a low ridge to scan the fresh ground on the far side. From where I was I could not see over it, but Macandrew stood and spied and then moved on again. It was as I came up to the crest that I saw the deer. They were a hundred yards or so away on our right, well up wind of us. Whether they had been there all along and Macandrew had missed them, or whether they had moved into view only after he had moved I could not tell. They were moving when I saw them. If they had not been, the chances are that I should not have seen them, because, as I say, I had rather left things to Macandrew and was not myself in a state of full alert. Anyhow, there they were, and they had not yet seen us.

I gave a long low whistle. The deer would hear it, of course, but anything is better on the hill than the human voice, and a whistle is not easy to identify, or even to place accurately for direction. Macandrew stopped on the instant and turned. I pointed, and he gave one look and then moved steadily on again. This is the fruit of experience, and it is a thing the beginner finds very difficult to do. The beginner's instinct, when he is caught like this, is to stand still, or perhaps drop to the ground, but if you are in full sight of the deer, this does more harm than good. The sudden cessation of movement catches their eye, and awakens their suspicions, more than its steady continuation. The chances are that you have lost them anyway, but if you keep moving steadily until you are again out of their sight, there is always a possibility that they may let you go without themselves moving. Whether this is because they have not in fact seen you, or whether a steady movement not in their direction does not alarm them, I have never been able to understand. At any rate, the proper course is to maintain your movement, and this, after the most momentary pause, Macandrew did. He moved ahead, not looking at the deer, and I followed him, not looking at them either. We moved on like this for perhaps twenty yards, taking the line which he knew, with his compulsive instinct for such things, would take us soonest into dead ground. Then he stopped, and I stopped behind him, and we both turned. Sure enough, the deer were no longer in sight, not because they had moved, but because we had put a fold of the ground between us and where they had been. Whether they were still there, of course, we had no means of knowing.

Still, they had been not far from us, and they might be the only deer we should see that day. The thing had to be tried. Macandrew cocked his rifle and I did the same. Then he motioned me to the right and forward, and he himself moved off to the left, still under the fold of ground. We were to try a quick stalk along the face and straight up into the wind, taking separate lines a little apart in case the deer moved sideways. I suppose Macandrew took the left because that was the up-hill side, and if the beasts moved, that was the direction they were likely to move in. I do not think this meant any doubts about my shooting. It was just that in a moment of quick decision he himself naturally took the best line for the beasts, and my supporting role on the right was then axiomatic. Not that I had any time to think about this, still less to feel any resentment. As so often happened, I suddenly found myself, after a period of suspended responsibility, out on my own, and with the success of the whole stalk in my hands. It needs only one false move by one man to wreck a whole stalk, just as it needs only one badly feathered blade to stop a whole boat's crew.

I got my head round the side of the fold, but could still see nothing. I began at once to think that the beasts had seen us and moved, but I had to go on as if they were still there. This agonisedly careful approach to beasts which may in fact be no longer there is a thing that happens to all stalkers at times. It calls for special concentration, because once you let the belief that they have moved grow on you, you are apt to get more careless in your own movements, or, worse, actually fail to see them in time if you do come up with them. With the deer on the hill you have to be consciously looking for them the whole time, and it is very difficult to look properly for something you do not believe is there.

I went on, taking the best line I could, but also moving

as fast as I could, because in the circumstances time was important. I must have made thirty or forty yards when I saw them. They were well up on a skyline, but away over to my left and moving further away up hill. They were not running, but moving a little uncertainly, stopping occasionally to graze, but never for long, and then moving on again. They had certainly not seen either of us where we now were, but I thought they were a little disturbed, and had made up their minds it was time to be gone. I could have got a shot, but it would have been a long one, and the trouble was, they were already in Macandrew's ground and not mine. For all I knew, he might well be much more up to them than I was, but not yet quite ready to fire, and if I fired from where I was, they would not, in their present mood, give him a chance, but would be off at once. I have said that in the shooting of the hinds you take a safe shot as soon as you see one, without waiting for the other man, but here my shot would not be all that safe, whereas Macandrew's might. And the truth is that I was still labouring to some extent under my earlier sense of guilt, and I was afraid I might not shoot well. I got my sights on a suitable beast, but hesitated, and the beast moved on again.

After that one hesitation I was indeed lost. I resigned my responsibility, stayed where I was and left it to Macandrew. I simply lay there watching them, and all the time they drifted steadily up the hill away from me, and still Macandrew did not fire. This all takes a bit of explaining, but in fact it happened in no time at all, a matter almost of seconds rather than minutes. I do not know how long it was before I faced the fact that the beasts had gone too far now even for Macandrew, and that the shot I ought to have taken had probably been our one chance at this herd, and for all I knew our one chance for the day. When I did face it, my heart sank. I had started the day on the wrong foot, and now I was in worse trouble than ever. Of course my offence could not be brought home to me. No one could prove that I had had a shootable beast in my sights and had not fired, but I thought that Macandrew, with his deadly eye for the ground, would know I must have. The beasts were well away now, still moving at their own pace, but quite out of reach. Once they start to move like that, they keep on moving, and to try to walk after them is about as much use as trying to run after a hare. I left my position and moved almost stealthily back along the line I had come. It was not the beasts I was dodging now, it was Macandrew. I did not want him to know how far up I had got. When I was back in low ground, I got to my feet and started walking back, and a moment later I saw him. He was standing under a small knoll, watching me. He did not move. I turned and walked towards him. There was nothing else I could do, but I would as lief have faced a firing squad.

He looked grim. Of course it was not only me he was angry with. He was too just a man, and knew too much of the game, for that. I still did not know his part in it, and certainly could not ask him, but the fact remained that we had muffed it between us. We had been up to the deer, and the deer still did not know it, and we had not fired a shot between us. He said, 'Could you no shoot?'

I shook my head. 'Not safely,' I said. I had an urge to say that I had thought they were his beasts, but this would have been to confess too much of the truth.

He looked at me very straight. 'I had thought you could have,' he said. I shook my head again. 'I could no get up to them,' he said, 'not at all, without shifting them. I left it to you.'

The urge to say I had left it to him was almost irresistible now, but again I resisted it. 'I'm sorry,' I said.

'Och well,' he said, ' 'twas you that saw them. I was for

going by them when you stopped me.' This was deliberate kindness, and a measure of the man's greatness, but it made me feel worse than ever. I smiled at him ruefully, but did not say anything. 'Och well,' he said again, 'where there's some, maybe there'll be others.' He uncocked his rifle and I did the same. Then he started off down the hill, and I went after him.

CHAPTER THIRTEEN

Kindness or not, the thing left Macandrew absolutely determined to redeem our performance before we went home. I was certainly not being deliberately punished for my failure to shoot, but I had cause to regret it more than once before the day was out. For the next four hours or so we walked incessantly, but saw practically nothing and never got a shot. Once we saw a string of beasts grazing on what looked to me an impossibly high skyline, but Macandrew set off walking determinedly up to them, even though my mind boggled at the thought of what the drag back would be like if we did get any of them. As it was, I need not have worried. The beasts moved long before we got up to them, and Macandrew gave up the attempt. They were all on the move all day, not really wild, as they can be sometimes, but restless and constantly changing their ground for no very good reason that was apparent.

Our only hope seemed to be to come on a herd pretty well by chance, as indeed we had the first time, and then to take a quick shot—the quick shot, I thought bitterly, which I ought to have taken the first time, and had not. This in fact is what we did, but not before it was so late in the day that I had begun to think that even Macandrew must soon concede defeat and make a move for home. We were moving down to the track at a point away out near the eastern marches of the estate when we suddenly saw a smallish herd lower down on the face. What they were doing there was no more explicable than any of the deer's other movements during the day, but there they were, actually below us, so that in going up to look for beasts on the higher parts of the face we had somehow managed to get down-wind of them.

I have said that Macandrew was a deliberate, almost stately mover, but now he went into action with the speed and ruthlessness of a paratrooper. He said, 'Och, come on, now,' and went straight down the bank at our feet, slithering and bumping his way among the projecting boulders until he was in the dead ground at the bottom. I followed him, jerked out of my settled gloom by his galvanic activity, and in the more calculating part of my mind comforted by the thought that from here to the track was only a short haul, and all downhill. I kept an eye on the beasts until my head went under the line of sight, but they showed no sign of having seen us. I said so to Macandrew as I came down alongside him, but he said, 'Och, the hell with that, we'll no give them time to think.' He cocked his rifle sharply, and was off running, actually running, across the stretch of low ground that lay between us and the ridge above the beasts. I cocked my rifle and went after him, feeling suddenly that I was struggling in the wake of a younger and keener man. I suppose the frustration had been building up in him all day, so that when the late chance came, everything went by the board but the energy and expertise of the professional killer. It was a wholly new picture of him, and slightly disturbing, but I was too busy keeping up with him to dwell on it.

I did not in fact keep up with him in the strictly physical sense. He reached the ridge several yards ahead of me and flung himself straight into the firing position. I threw myself down beside him, but he had fired before I got my rifle up. It only lasted a few seconds, those few fatal seconds during which the deer hesitate when they are shot at and try to locate the source of the danger instead of simply running from it. I think we each fired three times, though my third shot was, as so often with my last, an unnecessary coup-de-grace at a beast which was already dead on its feet. We got three shootable beasts before the rest started to run, and Macandrew with his last brought down a calf that was hesitating, the way they do, beside the fallen hind. It was not shooting as I like to think of it, but it was quick professional work, effective and, as far as it allowed of mercy, not unmerciful.

When it was all over and the beasts had vanished, we lay there for a second or two in the sudden enormous silence, both recovering our breath and both, I think, momentarily swamped by the characteristic reaction of slightly woe-begone relief, that is so curiously like a man's reaction to the successful consummation of the act of love. Then Macandrew got up, first on to his knees and then on to his feet, with all his old deliberation of movement suddenly returned to him. He turned to me, looking at me with an almost shy smile as he automatically uncocked his rifle. 'Och well,' he said, 'it's been no so bad a day at that.' Then we got on with the work.

We were well beyond the burn here, and the Landrover was away to the west of it, where we had left it when we had last taken to the higher ground. We had crossed the burn higher up, stepping from stone to stone among the rushing water, and from what I had seen of it, there did not look to be over much water coming down. It had stopped raining early the night before, nearly twenty-four hours ago now, and the water runs off the hill very quickly. I thought the car would manage the ford all right. We each dragged a beast down to the track, and then I said,

'Shall I go and get the car, or shall I bring the other beast down?'

He did not hesitate at all. 'Do you get the car,' he said. 'I'll manage the beast.' Of course the walk up the hill and the drag back was the harder job of the two, but I did not think he was considering me in the matter. I thought that the one job simply came more naturally to him than the other. When you came to think of it, to go back up the face, at the end of a day like that, and drag down a second heavy beast was prodigious labour for a man of his age, but it was labour he was used to and took for granted. It would be driving the Landrover through the ford he would not like, and he was as happy to leave that to me as I was to leave the beast to him. I nodded, slung my rifle on my shoulder and set off along the track.

Neither job, in fact, gave any trouble. There was plenty of water at the ford, and going fast because here it was unimpeded, but a Landrover is a heavy vehicle and has plenty of clearance. I brought her jolting and bouncing over the rounded stones that formed the bed, with the engine roaring in low gear and the water sluicing sideways under her, and got to Macandrew just as he was pulling the dragging rope out of the third beast's neck. We loaded the three and put the tail-board up on them, and then he put his rifle in the rack, where mine already was, and climbed heavily into the nearside seat. He did not say anything. I took the wheel again and set course for home. It was only after we had negotiated the ford and were going steadily westwards along the track that I remembered my faulty car.

It was getting dark now, but it was not yet really late as the working day goes. I thought there would still be someone at Davie Bain's garage, and I thought that by the time we had finished in the larder Macandrew would certainly not fancy having to drive me home. As soon as we got into the yard, I tried the car, in case the drier weather had helped, but there was not a spark in her. I told Macandrew, and he said he would go into the lodge and phone. 'They'll be here before we're through with the beasts,' he said, and I knew this could be true. It was no great distance, and you could drive faster over that road in the dark, because the hazard was always the unseen car round the next bend, and at night you had the lights to warn you.

I said, 'Tell them to bring a spare coil. I think that's what we want.'

He nodded. 'I'll do that,' he said. He vanished into the lodge, and I switched on the larder lights and began the unloading of the beasts.

He was soon back. 'They'll be over,' he said, and then we put on our aprons and got started on our butcher's chores. We worked two on a beast, one at each end. There was only the one bench, and in any case that is the quickest and most efficient way to work. When you are on your own, the great, inert carcass is apt to slew sideways on the bench and make clean work very difficult. The deer, like most running animals, is a narrow beast, for all its size and weight, and has no flat back to speak of. That is also the reason why you never shoot at a beast unless you have a full broadside view of it. If you shoot to any degree from the front or rear, you are apt to wound it in any one of a number of ghastly ways without killing it or even bringing it down. I have often had a beast in my sights for minutes on end, and finished by letting it go, because it has never, as it grazed, turned fully sideways on to me.

We worked silently in the yellow glare of the bulb in the roof, both knowing what we had to do and each intent on his own work, while the windows under their wire gauze coverings turned full black as the darkness deepened outside. We had got the second beast finished and hanging

134

from its pulley, and were getting the third on to the bench, when we heard the sound of a car in the yard, and saw the lights flicker momentarily across the windows as it swung round and came to a halt. We did not stop our work. I think we were both, though we would not admit it, getting near the limits of our physical endurance, and had no clear idea left in us but to get on and finish for the day. I suppose I expected someone to come to the door of the larder and speak to me about the car, but no one came. There was no reason, in fact, why they should. They knew my car well enough, and had been told what the trouble was. The lights outside were steady now, and I supposed whoever it was was working on my car by the light of his own headlamps.

I had my back to the window as I worked, but presently I saw Macandrew take his eyes for a moment off the bench and look out at the activity in the yard. Then he lowered his face and looked at me. I thought he looked a little oddly. 'You're honoured,' he said. ''Tis himself has come.'

'Davie?' I said, and he nodded.

'Ay, just,' he said, and we went on with our work.

We had got the third beast hung up, and were starting on the cleaning up, when I heard an engine cough in the yard and then roar into life. I knew it was my engine, not the engine of the car from the garage. I knew in my numbed mind that I should have to go out and talk to Davie Bain. I should have to leave Macandrew in the larder and go and talk to Davie alone, and I did not want to at all. I looked at Macandrew. 'He's got her started,' I said, 'I'd better go out and have a word with him.'

He looked at me, and for a moment we stared at each other in the yellow light of the larder. We had exhausted our bodies in company, and now the barrier between our minds seemed very thin. 'Ay,' he said, 'you do that.' I turned and went to the door, and felt him watching me as I went.

The headlights of the garage car were still on. The bonnet of my car was down now, with the engine turning over quietly under it. Davie Bain stood with his back to it, half leaning on it, but still immensely tall in the white light of the lamps. I went across to him. He watched me come, but did not move. I said, 'That's very good of you, Davie. She'll be all right now?'

He straightened up slowly. Then he put a hand in through the driving window and switched off the engine. There was no sound anywhere now, only the steady white light in which we both stood.

'Ay,' he said. 'I put a new coil in. She'll be all right.' I was going to thank him again when he cut me short. 'I was wondering,' he said, 'would you be a friend of Miss Allison's, now?'

I suppose, so far as I reasoned the thing at all, I thought he could not know or he would not have asked. But I am not pretending I did much reasoning, or was in any state to do it. I said, 'Allison? No. I know there was a Jimmy Allison used to work in the glen at one time. Would she be any relation?'

He stared down at me, and I gave him back stare for stare. Even in that white light you could see how red he was. 'Ay,' he said, 'his sister.' Then his eyes shifted, and I turned and found Macandrew standing just behind me. I hardly looked at his face, but I was aware at once of an enormous antagonism between the two men, the sort of intense personal antipathy which in private matters only the Highlands seem any longer to have time for.

I said, 'Davie's asking about Jimmy Allison, Mr Macandrew.'

Macandrew said nothing. That was the unnerving thing.

The two men were of a height, both a head taller than I was, and they stood there looking at each other over my head, and neither of them said a word to the other. I turned to Macandrew again. I said, 'Had Jimmy Allison a sister?'

Macandrew took his eyes off Davie and looked at me. His face looked very old in that light, and as hard as granite. He said, 'Mr Bain should know well, I'm thinking.'

Only then Davie moved. He stood clear of my car and turned towards the car he had come in. It was a service car belonging to the garage, not his own. 'Och well,' he said, 'I just wondered.' Then he turned and went to the car, and a moment later the lights went out, and the yard was in darkness except for the yellow glow from the gauze-covered windows of the larder. As Macandrew and I stood there, the engine started, and then the lights went on again. The car moved at once. It swung round in a slow arc, so that we saw it only from the near side. We knew Davie Bain was in the driving seat, but we could not see him. Then the car gathered way and turned out of the yard, and we saw its lights heading down the road towards Bridge of Eilean.

Macandrew said, 'Yon's an ill man,' and then we went back to the larder and finished what we had to do. We neither of us said a word to each other the whole time.

Only when I was ready to go I said, 'Will you be going out tomorrow?'

'I will not,' he said. 'Do you please yourself. The car will be here if you want it.'

I did not know whether I should or not. I nodded, and we said good night, and I started the car without trouble and headed for home.

There was a letter for me on the floor of the porch when I opened the door. It would have come by post, which meant it would have been brought by the bus at tea-time, along with the daily paper, which had been folded tight and forced through the letter-box after it. It was a plain buff envelope with a type-written address, but the stamp had the lion of Scotland on it and the postmark was Aberennan. Such letters as I had nearly all came from the south, and there was only one person in Aberennan I could expect to hear from. I took the envelope and the typewriting to be deliberately aimed at anonymity, and I was right, because the letter itself, when I took it out, carried the thing even further. It was a single slip of white paper, also typewritten. It was not signed. It just said, *Sunday, 09.00, Bunrathie,* and then, in brackets, the letters GR and the six figures of a map reference on the national grid.

I was pleased with my letter from Mary, much more pleased than I should have been with something more personal. I was pleased with the discretion of it. I did not mind the spy stuff, so long as it showed she was taking the thing seriously. I was pleased that she knew how to take off a six-figure map reference, though that went well enough with what I already knew of her. Above all, I was pleased with her assumption that I should know what it meant and be able to locate the reference on my own survey sheet. I unfolded my sheet and found Bunrathie at once. The name itself was marked. I took it to be a farm of sorts. It was south and a little west of Kinloch-eilean, well up on the south side of the glen, but itself in a small valley where a burn came down to the eastern end of the loch. I thought it was perhaps where she had left her car that first time, when she had come in along the high tops to get to the graveyard of the Maceacherns, un-less in her very well-considered caution she had varied even that. At any rate, I should be there at nine on Sun-day morning. My only problem was that to get there I had to go through Kinlocheilean. There was no avoiding this at all. I thought I should have to do that very early in the

morning, perhaps even before daylight. I did not want anyone to see my car going through. For one unhappy moment
it occurred to me to wonder whether Davie Bain had not
been at pains to see that I had the use of the car at the
week-end. I did not really think this was so. I thought he
had come out to Ardevie himself because he had a question to ask me. All the same, the idea was one I did not
like. I burnt the letter and the envelope, and had my
supper and went to bed.

CHAPTER FOURTEEN

I did not go out on the Saturday. I was very tired, and the day before had left a very slightly sour taste in my mouth. There was a sheer disinclination to go through it all again, especially with the additional burden of being on my own. I enjoyed being on my own if I was up to it, but it takes a lot more out of you. I rationalised my mere reluctance by telling myself that if I went out, I might not do much good, and I was not justified in charging Mr Sinclair for what might be less than a full day's work. And there was another consideration. I was in for a long day on the hill on Sunday. I hoped it would not involve any undue excitement, but it would certainly involve a lot of walking. I might as well rest while I had the chance, and from a purely practical point of view I needed one day in the week at home to keep abreast of my household chores.

So I did my Sunday jobs on the Saturday. Physically they were not very strenuous, and mentally they were at least semi-automatic. While I was doing them I thought at intervals about Davie Bain. The curious thing is that I did not really know how seriously I ought to take him. In himself he frightened me, and I had no doubt at all that he was potentially dangerous. As Macandrew had said, an ill man. But I did not know, in the present circumstances, how dangerous he actually was, to me or to Mary Allison.

This was because I did not know what was at stake. I expected, and certainly hoped, to know this better by some time on Sunday afternoon, but at the moment I knew very little. I knew he was a crook, and by local standards a master crook. But I did not see him as a Professor Moriarty, nor did I suppose that he had his spies in every corner of the glen. I had met Mary three times, apart from my visits to the bank, and he did not seem to know of any of our meetings. On the whole I put him down as a local crook, baffled in some piece of local crookery, and angry and puzzled at his bafflement. He was ready to have my cottage searched on the sly and to arrange a burglary at Mary's flat, but he was not above coming all the way over from Kinlocheilean to ask me, point blank, what he badly wanted to know. He seemed to be thrashing about in his anger and bafflement rather than laying highly organised plots to overcome it. But I still did not know how angry he was, or how much the whole thing really meant to him.

It was only later in the day that another idea occurred to me, and this worried me a good deal. I wondered whether he had come over to Ardevie, not to find out if I was in touch with Mary, but because he knew I was and wanted to see if I would deny it—and deny it, in particular, to him. The point was this. Because of what had happened at the graveyard the last time I had gone there, I had identified him, almost from the start, as the enemy I had to deal with. But he could not know I had identified him, and he had every reason to suppose, what was true, that Mary had not identified him at all. I wondered now whether in my exhaustion and confusion of the evening before I had not, after all, done the wrong thing. If I had admitted, quite casually, to knowing Mary, he might at least have supposed that I did not connect him in any way with her affairs. But I had made, as far as I had been up to it, a fairly elaborate pretence of not knowing her, and I had even in the course of it let him know that I knew of Jimmy's existence, which, now that I came to think of it, I had on the face of it very little reason for doing. If I was wrong in supposing that he did not know of my meetings with Mary, or if at least he had his reasons for suspecting that I was in touch with her, my denial would certainly tell him a good deal. I was in fact faced with the unwelcome possibility that he had come over to Ardevie to find out one thing, and that he had indeed found out precisely what he had wanted to know.

I hardly went out of the house all day, and got to bed early because I had decided to be up early next morning. I had no doubt now that the best thing was to get through Kinlocheilean before daylight. With the days as short as they were, this did not in fact mean leaving more than an hour or so earlier than I should anyhow have done. My appointment was for nine, and I am the sort of man who would always rather have time to spare than have to hurry. And there were good reasons, in fact, for giving myself plenty of time. I had my road to Bunrathie worked out on the map, but where side-roads and lanes are involved it is not always easy to get it right the first time on the actual ground. Also, I did not want to leave my car too near the place of meeting. After our meeting at the Yetts, I thought it very likely that the same idea would occur to Mary, but so long as we were not both so clever that we tried to leave our cars in the same place, it would be better if both of us got to Bunrathie on foot. So as I say I got to bed early. It was only when I was in bed and conditioning myself to sleep that Davie Bain gave me his final fright for the day.

I suddenly wondered if he could in fact have seen Mary's letter. The letter had come through the post, and unless you live in a James Bond world, you assume as a matter of course that your letters reach you unopened. The days of the village postmistress, with her steam kettle always on the hob, are no longer with us, and the postman covering a wide area in his little red van has not the same interest in local affairs. But my letters did not reach me by post because, red vans or no red vans, actual postal deliveries did not extend this far along the glen. Letters reached Kinlocheilean by post and came on, under a Post Office contract, by bus. And the bus service, like so many other local concerns, was owned and run by Davie Bain. I did not know how the thing worked, and until now I had not thought of it. I had been told when I got here that letters and newspapers and almost anything else you ordered came out on the bus, and so I found they did, and so now as a matter of course I accepted that they should. Only up to now I had never supposed that Davie Bain or anyone else, even in the intense, in-grown world of Gleneilean, would be sufficiently interested to want to read my post, what there was of it. The bus driver was a ginger-haired youth called Angus, who was friendly and obliging enough. But he was an employee of Davie's, and I did not know what happened to the mail between the time it left the Post Office and the time it left Kinlocheilean on the bus.

Then I told myself it was all nonsense. I was making a bugbear of Davie again, which I was too apt to do after any meeting with him, because the man himself frightened me so. And in any case the letter had been anonymous and as discreet as its purpose allowed. All the same, I wished, not for the first time since the thing started, that I was on the telephone. I did not think I could suspect even Davie of tapping telephones. I put the thing out of my mind, and managed, though not immediately, to get to sleep.

It was very cold when I got up. It was blowing harder than ever from the north, but the cloud cover seemed continuous. I could not see a star anywhere. I thought if this went on, we should have snow again before long. I could only hope it would hold off during the day. Snow can fall very heavily at that time of the year, even if it is not going to lie, and in what we had to do snow would be, to put it no higher, a very considerable complication. But I do not think it was really practical considerations that weighed with me. I had been looking forward to the day for more than one reason, and now suddenly, in this cold blackness and under this murky sky, my heart sank. I do not know any country as subject to the weather as the Highlands. The whole feel and character of the place, and even its actual appearance, change with the changing sky, and the sky can change very quickly. There are times when you want nothing more than to be out in the middle of this vast splendour, and merely to be there is a conscious exhilaration, and there are other times when you can hardly bring yourself to go out of the house, the outside world seems so full of menace. And yet in most cases the menace is not a physical one, any more than the exhilaration is. It is the country itself acting directly on your spirits, and it is largely the weather that determines how it shall act.

I took all sensible precautions. I dressed as warmly as I could, with my flask in my inside pocket and food in the others. I wore shoes for the drive, but put my boots in the car for the walk. I took a stick, which I do not usually carry, for myself and a second one for Mary in case she had not thought to bring one. I told myself, and took it for granted, that I was not embarking on anything physically dangerous. And yet when I had turned the lights out and locked the house behind me, I went into the bitter, blustering darkness full of an apprehension I could not shake off. I could not even see the country yet, but I felt it all round me, very empty and menacing, and I did not think that when daylight did come, it would do much to raise my spirits.

Thanks to Davie Bain, the car started first go. I had a picture of him learning on the Friday of my anonymous appointment and then, in the evening, when he got Macandrew's phone call, hurrying over to Ardevie to confirm, if he could, that my appointment was with Mary and to ensure that so far as the car was concerned I should be able to keep it. It was not after all as far-fetched as I had told myself the night before. It involved an assumption about the actual handling of the mail at Kinloch-eilean which might or might not be justified, but given that assumption it made sense without making a Professor Moriarty of him. If it was true, all my efforts to creep through Kinlocheilean before daylight were useless. All Davie had to do was to be somewhere about Bunrathie at nine o'clock and await events.

All the same, I drove fast, as I have said you could in darkness so long as you knew the road. My headlights swung to and fro between the water and the hill-face as the car swept round the bends. The water looked dark and threatening, breaking short and sharp on the rocks of a lee shore. Any sort of a wind puts up a nasty little seaway on a confined water like this. Whatever his needs of the moment, I always thought the chief of Ulva's isle ought to have known better than to take Lord Ullin's daughter out on it. It was as the car came round a left-hand bend that the lights suddenly picked out, standing up in flood-lit silhouette against the breaking water, the graveyard of the Maceacherns. I had not thought much of the grave-yard recently, and now, in my uncertainty and apprehension, the sudden momentary sight of it shook me. I remembered those few horrifying seconds when I had run in through the open gateway, expecting for no reason at all to find Mary spreadeagled on one of the gravestones. It

145

was gone, of course, almost as soon as I had seen it. The car turned, the lights swung and the thing was lost again in the darkness. But I wished I had not seen it. I all but wished I had not gone there in the first place.

It was still quite dark when I passed through Kinloch-eilean. I did not have to go through the middle of it. The village stood impaled on the narrow eastern end of the loch, and my road took me only through its southern outskirts. I could not see a light or a sign of life anywhere. It was no longer very early, but it was a Sunday morning. The place crouched in the darkness, giving nothing away. Once it was behind me, I let the speed down and started to think what I had to do. I was now heading for the main road, and well before I got there I had to find a side turning on my right, making southward up the side of the glen. It would only be a small road, and I was not sure from the map how it would be sign-posted, but it was the only one on that side, and it had looked to be a mile or so outside Kinlocheilean. I drove slowly now, watching the side of the road, and knew as I watched it that it was starting to get light. When I looked at my watch, I saw that it ought in fact to have been starting to get light well before this. Even when daylight of a sort emerged, the sky was going to be as dark as pitch.

My lights picked up the white finger-post before I saw the turning itself. It had some other name on it, not Bun-rathie, but this must be the one. I assumed that later Mary would come to it from the opposite direction, after driving north from Aberennan along the main road. Unless, that was, she had some other way to Bunrathie from further east along the glen. I eased the car into the turning and found myself on a narrow ribbon of rough tarmac between dry-stone walls. I drove very slowly for a quarter of a mile or so, and then stopped and got the map out. I thought I was on the right road. If I was, there should be another lane, even smaller, going off again to the right, and going, as far as I could see, straight past Bunrathie. I put the map away and drove on. The turning came about where I expected it. It was not all that much smaller, but it had fields on both sides of it, and it sloped upwards much less steeply than the lane I was now on. I thought this would be the beginning of the small valley where Bunrathie lay, and the farm itself should not be more than another quarter of a mile away. It was time I was looking for somewhere to put the car, but it was still not half light, and it was difficult to decide anything until I could see more of the whole lie of the country. I thought in the meantime I might as well try to locate the farm. I turned into the lane and pulled the car off to the side of it, with two wheels on the grass. Then I stopped, turned the lights out and got out.

I had forgotten how cold it was. It is so easy to do this inside a heated car. I believe a lot of people, driving in cold clear weather, skid on invisible ice purely because they have lost their apprehension of the cold outside. Now the wind was on me at once, full of that dank, penetrating cold which means that snow is coming and goes out of the air almost the moment the snow is down. There was still no snow falling, but I thought it could not be far off. I buttoned my coat at the neck and pulled my cap down on my forehead. Then I tilted my head to the wind, as you do instinctively if it is sharp enough, and set off along the lane.

Most of the farms in Scotland have their names on a board at the side of the road. It is part of the openness of the Scottish character, which lacks the southern farmer's almost febrile sense of privacy and independence. They do not call themselves This Farm or That Farm, I suppose because the Gaelic place-names themselves were originally descriptive of the place, though few people now know what they mean. I thought with any luck Bunrathie would identify itself when I came to it. I did not have any real doubt that I was where I had to be, but it was the sort of day, and I was in the sort of mood, when you want every assurance you can get. It did, sure enough. I saw the board in the grey light, and went close enough to read the name. The farm buildings were further back. They had lights on, and you could still see them in the murk, even at that distance. I turned, tilted my head the other way against the wind, and walked back to the car.

I could see the country well enough now, and I could not see any effective cover for a car anywhere. There were next to no trees, and the stone walls between the fields were no more than chest high. Finally I backed the car out into the bigger lane, drove it fifty yards or so beyond the Bunrathie turning and parked it as near in to the wall as I could get. Like that it did not in itself point to Bunrathie, and at least it was not in anyone's way. It was then a quarter past eight. I sat in the car for half an hour. Then I got out, put my boots on, took both my sticks, locked the car and set out again for Bunrathie.

As I came to the board, a figure came out of a gateway along the lane and came to meet me. She was dressed for the weather, all right, hooded in some sort of anorak, and wearing tight thick trousers with boots under them. She had no stick, and I was glad I had brought one for her. She said, 'It's a horrible morning. Will your car be all right?'

'The best I can do,' I said. I held out the stick to her. 'Will you take it?' I said. 'You may need it later. But I'll carry it for the time, if you like.'

She took it. 'Oh yes,' she said, 'thank you. I was wishing I'd thought of bringing one.'

I said, 'Do you know your way from here?' She nodded. 'All right,' I said, 'lead on, then, and I'll follow.' She

148

turned and started off, and I went after her. It must have been almost exactly nine o'clock, and still no more than half light.

CHAPTER FIFTEEN

Now that we had kept our appointment and were off on our walk, my mind should have been easier, but it was not. I was still worried about the weather, wondering, not whether it would snow, but when and how heavily. It was in fact a perfectly reasonable thing to worry about, though not to get in a fright over. Heavy snow on the hill gets at you in two ways. While it is falling it can curtail your field of vision and upset your sense of direction, and once it is down it makes the going treacherous and of course much more laborious. It also occurred to me to wonder whether, if the snow was down by the time we got there, Mary would still be able to find what she was looking for. Unless you have the experienced stalker's eye for the ground, it is in my experience quite extraordinarily difficult, even in the best of conditions, to find your way to an exact spot on the hill which you think you have marked down. Even if you have taken a long shot at a beast and seen it fall, and still more if it has run after you have hit it and then fallen, still within your field of vision, but at some distance from you, it is only quite seldom that you can walk straight on to it. In nine cases out of ten you get to where you thought it was, and then have to cast about over quite a wide area before you actually come on it. In theory, of course, you can fix your eyes on the spot where it has fallen and follow your eyes until you get there, but in practice this is hardly ever possible. For one thing you cannot walk on the hill without paying fairly close attention to the ground immediately in front of you, and for another the country is so broken that at some point of your walk, and probably at more than one, you will lose sight of the spot you are aiming at. You make your way round some obstacle, or go down into a bottom and then get up on to higher ground again, and pick up, or hope you are picking up, the line you were walking on. But you are lucky if it is in fact exactly the same line, and if it is not, the further you go on from there, the more the degree of error is magnified.

Mary was not walking to a spot she had just marked down within her field of vision. She was setting out to walk several miles to a spot she had marked down several weeks before. And the thing she was looking for was not a deer lying on the face of the hill (though even that is difficult enough to see), but a small box presumably earthed in under the peaty soil, or at least hidden in some way from casual observation. I had the greatest respect for her intelligence and resolution, but I wondered whether even she realised what she was up against. If in addition to all this the whole face was going to be under several inches of snow by the time we got there, the thing would be immeasurably more difficult, not only because the actual spot would be covered, and perhaps any marks she had put there, but also because lying snow can to a startling degree change the whole look and shape of the ground. However, there she was, going steadily and confidently ahead of me, and there was nothing I could do but follow her. Certainly the worst thing I could do would be to sow the seeds of doubt in her mind by voicing my own doubts now.

As for the difficulties or dangers which the snow might

bring on us during our walk, these were worrying rather than frightening. The great thing was that there were two of us. It is the solitary walker on the hill who is vulnerable in bad conditions, and I could not be sufficiently thankful that Mary had brought me along with her, even if it was Davie Bain and his burglary that I had to thank for it. For the rest, we were moving westwards along the hill face, presumably in a gradually descending line, with the road, at any rate after the first few miles, lying along the bottom of the face roughly parallel with our line. If things for any reason got really difficult, we might not find it possible to retrace our steps and get back to our cars, but we could at any point turn and go straight down the face, knowing that the comparative safety of the road lay at its foot.

The odd thing is that I was so taken up with the natural difficulties that I almost lost sight of the possibility of human intervention. I think if I had had any clear picture in my mind of the form this might take, I might have been more actively apprehensive, but I had not. If we had once got the box, I should have felt the immediate danger of an attempt to take it from us, and should have been concentrating on frustrating it. But even on the most optimistic view we were a long way from the box yet, and it would serve no one's purpose to interfere with us. The snow has no purpose to be served, and would interfere whether we had the box or not. For the moment the snow was the enemy, not Davie Bain.

But still the snow did not fall. Overhead the cloud cover was slate grey and northwards it was almost a cobalt blue, but it went on driving over us and did not drop its burden. I think in fact we were saved at first by our position fairly low down on the side of the glen. The mountains lay south of us, and where we were the wind was already starting to rise to them. The snow fell first, as it always does, on the highest tops, and then worked its way down to the lower ground. It had probably been falling on the peaks before daybreak, and the snowline was all the time moving down on us as we walked westwards, but it did not reach us till a good deal later.

The fields did not last long. I think it was only the valley that was fenced and cultivated, and we were soon out of that and on to the open hill-face. As I had expected, Mary began to edge northwards down the face, but our main direction was still west. She went with a commendable caution, using her stick in her right hand to steady her against the slope, although the wind itself helped us there. All the same, she set a steady pace and took what seemed to me a good line, so that after a bit I gave up trying to pick our line ahead and found myself following her as unquestioningly as I followed Macandrew. On our left the hill-face towered black over us, and on our right the glen spread its huge obscurity beyond the leaden streak of the loch, and low over everything the dark skies streamed southward on the wind. There was no forestry below us yet, and the face still fell fairly gently to the water. Presently, as we got further west, the lower face would take its sudden sharp plunge, and the forestry would start, and we should no longer be able to see the loch under it. Then, as far as I knew, we should be on Ardevie ground, but at the moment I was still in unfamiliar territory.

We walked steadily for perhaps an hour and a half, hardly speaking to each other at all. This may have been partly because when you are walking one behind the other conversation is not easy and does not come naturally. But I think mainly we were both preoccupied, with our minds concentrated almost exclusively on what we had in hand. I do not mean on the actual business of walking, which needed no particular concentration in these conditions, but on what we had come for and what we expected to make of it. For all I knew, Mary may already have been worrying about finding her cache again, with the day as dark as it was, and the snow threatening, though she did not say so. All I know is that we walked on in silence, I think very much aware of each other and glad of each other's company, but neither of us willing either to say what was in our minds or to talk of anything else.

After about an hour and a half I called a halt and suggested a rest and something to eat. It must have been a long time now since either of us had breakfasted, and we were using up a good deal of energy. She agreed, but I thought not very willingly, and we sat for a few minutes with a rock between us and the wind, and ate biscuits and chocolate. What we should both have liked was something hot to drink, but this cannot really be managed on the hill. A vacuum flask is too fragile and bulky, and any sort of heating gear too cumbersome. The stalkers brew a fearful sort of tea—they call it drumming up—by hanging a tin can over a heather fire and scattering tea-leaves and sugar on the smoky water, but for myself I would much rather drink water if I am thirsty (there is water everywhere, of course) and keep my flask for more solid comfort in an emergency. I said, 'How are we doing?'

She said, 'All right, I think. As soon as we see the trees, we'll go down to them and work along their top edge. We'll get some shelter there, anyhow.' She looked up at the dark, hurrying sky. 'Do you think the snow will hold off?'

'To be honest,' I said, 'I'm surprised it's held off as long as it has. And thankful, of course. I think we'll get it before we're home.'

She nodded. 'So do I,' she said. 'Shall we go on, do you think?'

'If you're ready.'

She said, 'I'd rather be on the move.' She sounded uncertain and edgy, more than I had ever heard her, but still determined.

'All right,' I said. 'You do what you want,' and we got up and were on the move again.

I do not know how long it was after that that we saw the dark line of the trees ahead of us and lower down, but as soon as we saw them, we headed down towards them. I suppose it was because we should soon be on Ardevie ground that about then I began to wonder if there were any deer on the hill. There was no logic in this, because the deer know no boundaries, but I think I wondered whether just because I was on Ardevie without a rifle I should see them everywhere. It is the sort of half-superstitious thing you do find yourself thinking about the deer. I have even heard people maintain that they know when you are not out after them, and do not mind showing themselves. I do not think I really believe this, though there may be something in it. All animals see more in the movements and attitudes of other creatures than the human mind, so long dependent on verbal communication, can ever compass. That is what people mean when they say that their dog understands every word they say to it. It is not, of course, the words the dog understands, but the unconscious physical signals that still go with them. It may well be that to animal eyes hunting man shows that he is hunting by the way he moves. At any rate, as we came down towards the edge of the trees, I began, no more than half consciously, to keep an eye out for deer on the hill-face above us. I still do not know what would have happened if I had not.

I did not see any deer, whether or not there were any there. I did not, of course, look for them at all carefully or systematically. You cannot do this over one shoulder while you are moving on the hill, especially if you are moving at someone else's pace. But I did occasionally, when I thought about it and had the attention to spare, throw a quick glance up the face on our left, looking for the familiar pattern of shapes and above all for any movement. It was after we had come above the trees and levelled out on a line twenty or thirty yards higher up that I did see movement. It was only for a split second. Something moved on a crest, dark against a temporarily lighter background, and then stopped moving. I did not know whether it had dropped under the crest, or whether I had lost it because it stopped moving. But I knew, even though I could no longer see it, that it was not deer. It was just something moving on the hill that was not part of the hill. Also I thought it had stopped moving, or dropped under the crest, as my head came round towards it, and that is a purely human trick.

I did not look up again after that. I could not have seen anything if I had, and above all I did not want to show any sign of interest. I walked on behind Mary exactly as I had before, saying nothing, but suddenly conscious of my heart thumping in my chest, as you are sometimes when you first see the deer you have been long looking for. We went on so for another minute or two, and then I spoke. I spoke very deliberately and clearly, with my voice pitched so that Mary should hear it, even across the wind. I said, 'Don't stop and don't turn round. But listen very carefully.'

Just for a second she hesitated, but I knew I could trust her. She went on again steadily, but with her head very slightly turned, as if to make sure she would hear what I had to say. I said, 'When you are ready, you must stumble and fall. Then pretend you have hurt your ankle. Act it up as much as you can. Silent film stuff. I'll explain when I come up with you. Take your time, but as soon as you are ready, carry on.'

She gave no sign at all, except that her head was no

longer turned as it had been. She went on steadily for another twenty yards or so, and then down she went. It was a good fall, because it was exactly the way you do fall when you are moving sideways along a face. Her right foot seemed to slip and go from under her, and she went down sideways over it, and rolled over once before she lay still. I stopped in my tracks and then started towards her. I think I shouted something like, 'Are you all right?' It did not in fact matter what I said, but I was hamming it up too for all I was worth. Before I got to her, she got awkwardly to her feet, with one hand clutching her right knee, and then she collapsed and went down again.

She sat crouching where she had fallen, with both hands clutching her right ankle. She had her back to the hill. I came and knelt in front of her. She said, 'Can they hear us?' She spoke in a whisper.

I said, 'Not possibly,' but found I was whispering too.

'Where are they?'

'Up on the face behind you. Someone or something moving but keeping out of sight. I had to assume we are being watched. How far have we still to go?'

'I'm not sure, but quite a way. I haven't seen the marks yet.'

I said, 'Do you mind if I feel your ankle? Purely professional.'

'Go ahead,' she said. 'Ankles aren't what they were.' She seemed quite cheerful again now, as if the challenge had taken the uncertainty out of her. I think the wind and the dark sky and the threat of snow had been wearing her down, and perhaps as I say a nagging doubt of her own ability to find what she wanted when we got there. Now, given human opposition, she was a different creature. She was a bonnie fighter, was Mary. Meanwhile I pretended to examine the ankle, but there was no need to carry the pretence too far. She said, 'We'll have to go back?'

'I'm afraid so,' I said. 'I assume it's the box they want, not us. They've evidently been adding things up a bit. Tell me one thing. If we turn back from here, even if they assume we were on our way to it, they can't find it on their own?'

She shook her head quite decisively. 'Never in this world,' she said.

'Right,' I said. 'Then it's back to square one. We go back, slowly and painfully, because of your damaged ankle. They've no reason to think we've seen them. I imagine once we turn back, they'll let us go for now and wait for us to try again. Anyhow, that's the only assumption we can go on.'

She said, 'Yes, that makes sense. All right. Let's do a first-aid act and then start back.'

I bandaged her ankle elaborately with my scarf. I missed the scarf as soon as I took it off. No coat collar, however well designed and closely buttoned, ever fits tight to the neck, and that damned wind found the gap at once. If Mary's ankle had really been hurt, I should not have minded, but I grudged the loss of my scarf to satisfy the lurking watcher on the hill. When it was done, I helped her up. We mimed a bit of a consultation, and then set off back eastward, with her on my left, holding on to my arm, and our sticks in our outside hands. It was all fairly elaborate, and I wondered how long we had to keep it up. I hoped not for too long, because it was slow going, and we had to get home some time. In fact I need not have worried, or not about that. We had not been going ten minutes when the snow started.

It started as it always does, with a movement in the air, something half seen out of the corner of your eye, drifting down too slowly to be natural. After a moment you get a flake sharply focused as it falls, and then there are more of them, and in a moment or two you know what you are in for. We were still partly under the lee of the trees, and it was eddying down fairly gently, but I knew what it would be like when the fall got thicker, and we were out on the open face. The only compensation was that it would cut down the visibility considerably. Also, like the rain, it would be falling on the unjust as well as the just. I thought that with the snow falling on him, and no longer a clear sight of us, if any, and our expedition in any case clearly abandoned, our watcher would soon lose interest in us and start to find his own way home. Meanwhile, we had to get home ourselves, and I did not much fancy the prospect.

It was soon obvious that we could not go on as we were. It might be possible for one person to lean on another's arm going up-hill or down, but sideways along the face it cannot be done, because the two are as often as not walking on different levels. Even if Mary had been above me on the slope, the difference in our heights might have helped a bit, but she was below me, and if we were to keep up the act with any sort of conviction, this could not be changed. The whole charade had, literally, got off on the wrong foot. It seemed amazing, when I considered it later, that we had kept our act up as long as we did. Long before we got back to Bunrathie we were thinking only of keeping going, and in the right direction. In what style we managed it, or who saw us, had become altogether unimportant. In fact it was quite soon after we were clear of the trees that I took one look up the hill and then pulled Mary in under the partial shelter of a rock. 'Let's get that scarf off,' I said. 'I need it and you don't.' I did need it, in fact, because the snow was finding its way in with the wind, and I was in danger of getting wet from the neck down inside my clothes, which is the worst way of getting wet.

She stopped at once and unwound it. I shook the dry

snow out of it and put it back where it was needed. She said, 'Won't they see?' She still spoke quietly, even in that howling wilderness. The feeling of being watched conditions your behaviour compulsively in defiance of logic.

I jerked my head up the hill. 'Look,' I said.

The snow had shut down, of course. We could see with decreasing clearness for barely a hundred yards above us, but then a moving curtain of white intervened, and beyond it there was nothing, only further depths of whiteness. Our watcher had been much further up than that. The play was over, and we had other things to think about. Mary looked up and saw. 'Thank goodness for that,' she said. I was glad she was so cheerful about it.

'Right,' I said. 'Line ahead again. Will you lead or shall I?'

'What do you think?'

'On balance I'd rather you did, because you can make your own pace and count on me to keep up with you. If I go ahead, I may hold the pace down unnecessarily, and we need all the pace we can make. But if you find it a strain after a bit, let me know, and we'll change over.'

I knew at once that that was what she wanted. She was a girl who preferred leading to being led, and it was her line of country. She wanted me there, but it was support she wanted, not leadership. I did not mind this in the least, and from what I had seen she was unlikely to lead us wrong. All she said was, 'All right. Let's get on, then.' We moved out from behind our rock with Mary ahead, and from then on our only thought was to get back to Bunrathie.

It was a nasty walk, and it got nastier as the snow got deeper underfoot and our muscles lost their resilience, but we were in no real trouble as long as we both kept on our feet. If Mary had really fallen and hurt herself, it would have been bad, and still worse if I had, but neither of us did. I did in fact fall once, but I did not hurt myself, and I was on my feet and after her again before she knew I was down. She herself, after her one piece of play-acting, never fell at all.

I do not know how long the whole thing took. I did not look at my watch until much later, when I was back in my car and on my way home. Time was irrelevant so long as the daylight lasted, and unless we got seriously astray, there was enough of that left. It was when we came to the first wall that we knew we had managed it. After that it was only a matter of casting about until we found the lane. By the time we got into the lane there was much less snow coming down, and the wind was falling. I did not think we should have any trouble with the cars.

I said, 'I'll come with you to your car,' but she would not have that.

'Better not,' she said. 'I'll be all right once I'm on the road.' We stood there in the lane, very near where we had met in the morning. It seemed a long time ago now. 'What's the next move?' she said.

I shook my head at her. I think I had less left in me than she had. 'I don't know,' I said. 'I'll have to think. Can I phone you? I'll use a box. I don't want you to write.'

She thought. 'All right,' she said. 'Phone me on Thursday at about six. Reverse charges, and then you won't have to keep on fiddling with coins.' She gave me the number, and I made sure I had got it fixed in my mind.

I tried a last shot. I said, 'Can't you just leave the damned box where it is?'

'How can I?' she said. 'If you're right about today, they'd be after me sooner or later. You know that. I'd rather go back to the box with you at my back than with them.'

There was no arguing with this. The thing had gone too far now altogether. 'All right,' I said. 'I'll try to think of something, and phone you on Thursday. Are you sure you'll be all right?'

'Of course I'll be all right. That's if we got away with it today. They'll simply be waiting for me to try again.' She handed me the stick. 'Thank you for that,' she said. 'And for everything. Till Thursday, then.' Then she turned and went off down the lane, and I went back to my car and headed for home. I saw nobody all the way.

CHAPTER SIXTEEN

The next person I did see was Mr Sinclair, and he was in the yard at Ardevie when I got there next morning. I got out of the car and lifted the Mannlicher out of the back seat. He smiled when he saw it. 'All right,' he said, 'I haven't come to take my weapon back. I'm only up for a flying visit, in fact. How do you find her?'

'Beautiful,' I said.

He nodded. 'Macandrew says you're doing all right with her, so just keep on that way.' He was silent for a moment, looking at me. Then he said, 'Otherwise all well?'

It was the silence that did it. It made it difficult to take the question as a purely formal one. I thought it was a deliberate question, asked because there was something he really wanted to know. All the same, I answered it formally. I could not decide whether I wanted him to go on or not, but at least I knew that it was for him to make the running. I said, 'Yes, I think so, thank you.'

He nodded again. He was still looking at me, smiling a little now, as if he understood perfectly well what was in my mind, and did not hold it against me. He said, 'Macandrew tells me we've had Davie Bain over here.'

It was my turn to nod now. 'That's right,' I said. 'Friday evening, it was. I'd been having trouble with my car, and Macandrew phoned the garage when we got in.'

He said, 'That's pretty unusual, you know. I mean, Davie's coming himself like that. You'd have expected him to send one of the boys. It wouldn't matter what time it was. There are no problems with labour relations in Davie's business. If he told one of his chaps to come over at two in the morning, he'd be here.'

'Yes,' I said. 'Macandrew said I was honoured.' I hesitated a moment, and then offered him a pawn. I said, 'He seemed to think it a pretty doubtful honour.'

'He would,' he said. 'So should I. I don't have any dealings with Davie, bar the odd gallon of petrol if I'm caught short, and then I pay cash. Even that I avoid if I can. Of course my car's a bit of a special case. I take her to a man in Edinburgh.'

I said, 'I'm afraid mine hardly rates that. I get her serviced in Kinlocheilean. But I don't see more of Davie Bain than I can help, even so. I certainly didn't expect him over here the other evening. Or want him, if it comes to that.'

'No?' he said. 'No, Macandrew said you didn't seem too pleased to see him.'

He turned away from me now, and walked a few paces and then stopped. He had his head down and his hands in his pockets. It occurred to me that I had never seen him with his hands in his pockets before. It did not suit him. I thought he was making up his mind about something. Then he turned and came back to me.

'Look,' he said, 'it's no business of mine, and I'm sure you're quite capable of managing your own affairs. But I've been here longer than you have, and I hear a good deal one way and another, in and out of the glen. For what it's worth, my view of Davie is that he's pretty pure poison.'

'Yes,' I said. 'An ill man, Macandrew called him. I must say, he frightens me a bit. To meet, I mean.'

He shook his head. 'Macandrew wouldn't say what's in his mind,' he said. 'They none of them will. You ought to know that.' He stopped for a moment, looking at me. 'Especially if they think you're in any way involved with him. I don't mean on his side. I mean what I say, involved with him in any way. You must know what these people are like. They'll tell you anything, right or wrong, so long as it has no practical implications. If it has, they won't say anything at all.'

I said, 'Macandrew spoke of him in connection with a chap you had working here.'

He smiled, suddenly and disconcertingly, and shook his head. 'That's not the way Macandrew tells it,' he said.

For a moment I was genuinely puzzled. I said, 'But—' and he saw my confusion, and took me up on it.

'He says he mentioned Jimmy Allison to you one day. Just a casual reference. Then next day or some time you asked him about a connection between Jimmy and Davie, which he certainly hadn't mentioned. There had been one, of course. But it had all been before your time, so he wondered.'

I remembered now. I remembered my fishing question to Macandrew and the feeling I had had, even at the time, that you could not fish with Macandrew and get away with it. 'I see,' I said. I was wondering just what more I had to say when he came in again. I think he did it deliberately. Mr Sinclair had no more wish to cross-examine me than I had to be cross-examined by him.

He said, 'And then I gather when Davie was over here the other evening, it was Jimmy he was asking about. And of course that made Macandrew wonder still more.'

I said nothing because I still could not make up my mind what, if anything, to say. Then he said, 'You do understand, of course, there's no hostility in this? I mean, on Macandrew's side. Not to you. To Davie, yes, plenty. But he's a bit worried.'

I said, 'Yes, the hostility was obvious enough as soon as I saw them together.'

'Yes, well, it would be, of course. They're neither of them what you'd call talkative, but they don't hide their feelings much.'

'No indeed,' I said. I had made up my mind now. I was offering no information, even to Mr Sinclair, because it was not mine to offer, but I did not want to stop him talking.

For the second time I had the feeling that he knew the way my mind was working, and once again he smiled slightly, as if to make it clear that he accepted it without resentment. He said, 'Davie's got no police record. He poaches, of course, but only to please himself, in the way of sport, and he's not the only one who does that. Apart from that, no one knows anything for certain. But he's almost certainly got a finger in several pretty unsavoury pies, apart from his legitimate interests, and he's clever, and he's dangerous.' He stopped and looked at me very straight. 'I mean, really dangerous,' he said.

I said, 'I can believe that.'

'There was a man found dead up on Stravachie a few years back,' he said. 'Not a local. A travelling man, I think he was. Nobody knew much about him, but he'd been seen around. He'd been shot. All right, it was the stalking season, and there'd been some pretty wild shooting up there by London sportsmen, so it could have been an accident. By the time they found him, they couldn't be certain what he'd been shot with, or where the shooting had happened. There's the buzzards and the foxes, of course, and the Highland police aren't Scotland Yard, after all. But I was told they had the bullet out of him, and it didn't seem to come out of any weapon they knew of in these parts. Not a sporting rifle, anyway.'

I said, 'That wouldn't have stayed in him, probably. It would have gone straight through. Unless it was a spent one let off by one of your trigger-happy Londoners a mile or two away. What's the end of the story?'

'There isn't one. The chap wasn't a local, after all. You'd think someone must have known something, but no one was talking. Or not at the time. I heard things later. You know what it's like.'

'I can imagine. Where does Davie come in?'

'That's one of the things one heard afterwards. It was said that the chap had had dealings with Davie. Some people even said it was Davie who'd brought him here. And they may have fallen out over something. If you sup with the devil—you know? Maybe the chap's spoon wasn't long enough. No more than Jimmy Allison's was. He's in jail, the poor silly bastard, but at least he's safe there.'

It wasn't for me to bring him up to date on Jimmy Allison, and I let it go. I just nodded and said, 'I see.'

For a moment or two he looked at me, still smiling slightly. Then he shook his head. 'Well, that's all,' he said. 'You're no Jimmy Allison, I know that. But you aren't a local, either. Not yet, not by a long chalk. I don't want them to find you up on Stravachie with an unidentified bullet in you.'

I smiled back at him cheerfully. I did not feel cheerful in the least, but it was not in fact mainly myself I was worrying about. 'I'll do my best to stay alive,' I said. 'At least until we get the hinds in.'

'You do that,' he said. 'It's the hinds we want killed. I'll be off before you get back, and perhaps by the time I get back you'll be finished. Now you'd better go and find Macandrew. He'll be hovering somewhere, and I expect raring to go. Good luck to you, and blood on your knife.'

It is an old stalkers' valediction, though I always find it a rather disturbing one. I said, 'Thank you.' It seemed to cover everything. Then I went off to find Macandrew.

CHAPTER SEVENTEEN

Macandrew said, 'You were no out on the Saturday, then?'

I smiled at him a little defensively and shook my head. 'I was tired after the Friday,' I said. I did not say that I was at that moment even more tired after the Sunday. Sunday was my own affair, so long as I showed up for work on Monday, and there I was.

He was all consideration. 'Ay,' he said, 'just. There's no necessity at all to strap yourself.' He looked eastward out of the yard to the grey sky and the long white curve of the hill. 'The beasts will be down a wee with the snow lying,' he said. 'And the dragging will be easier. Och, we'll do fine yet.'

I hoped he was right. I had in fact a slightly stiff ankle, probably because of my fall on the walk back to Bun-rathie, though I had felt nothing at the time. I was determined it should not show, at least until we had been out on the hill long enough to justify it. In fact the chances were that after we had been out for a bit, it would loosen up, and I should no longer notice it myself. In the meantime I moved with a determined sprightliness, as if I had spent two days at home with my feet up.

The snow had stopped falling before I had got home the evening before, and the wind had gone down a lot, though it had stayed northerly. For the moment it had been less cold, but then it had got colder again during the night. The snow lay as it had fallen, and I thought there might be more on the way if the wind stayed where it was. I hoped that whatever there was would be gone by the week-end. I did not know yet what was to be done at the week-end, but I knew something must. If Davie Bain knew what I thought he did, the thing could not be put off indefinitely, or I was afraid what might happen. With her usual clear-sightedness Mary had seen the danger before I had. The enemy wanted their box. I still did not know how badly they wanted it, or what risks they were prepared to take to get it, but there remained the possibility that if she did not lead them to it of her own motion, they might try to make her, and that was a risk I could not take. The whole situation had closed in on us now, and some sort of a confrontation seemed inevitable. The thing was to bring it about as we wanted it and not as they did.

Left to myself, I should have had the police in on the thing before this, but I knew Mary would not, or not until she knew what was in the box, and I did not feel able to force her hand. For the matter of that, there was next to nothing even the police could do without her agreement. Neither they nor I could find the box, any more than Davie Bain could, unless she showed us where it was. The hill was too big and the box too small. I had some pointers to where about it might be (that was, if what Mary had said was right), and I could not find it in a month of Sundays. Nobody else had anything to go on at all. What it came to was that Mary had decided to handle the thing in her own way, and had asked me to help her on her own terms, and I had agreed to. If I did not like her terms, all I could do was opt out, and then I knew she would simply go on alone. When I phoned her on Thursday, all I could suggest, if I could think of it, was the safest way of doing what she wanted. It was no good suggesting her doing anything else. Meanwhile, the Ardevie hinds had to be shot, and I had promised Mr Sinclair to help with the shooting before I had promised Mary to help her get her damned box back. There was another week's work ahead of me, and from what I knew of Macandrew it would be a hard one.

The week started badly, because on that Monday for the first time I wounded a beast. Macandrew had got us up to a small herd on the lower slopes of Sronfiadh. I would maintain in self-defence that his final line was easier than mine, and he started shooting before I was ready. The only obvious shot for me was a big hind with a calf at foot, and for the reasons I have explained I shot the calf first. It went down all right, but by the time I had worked the bolt and got my sights on the hind, the deer had seen us and were beginning to run. My beast must have moved just as I fired, because I hit her hard and at the right height, but too far back. She staggered, and I thought she was going down, but before I could fire again, she had recovered herself and was off after the rest, not as fast as them, but too fast for me. I did try another shot at her as she went. Once a beast is wounded, you no longer observe the niceties. Your sole remaining purpose is to bring her down. But she was a difficult target by then, and I missed her altogether.

Macandrew had got two beasts and stopped firing. He saw what had happened, and there was no need for explanations. He came over to me, re-loading as he came. All he said was, 'You've but the two bullets left. Best re-load and we'll be after her. She'll no go far.'

'I'm sorry,' I said. 'I took the calf first, and she was off as I shot.'

'Och,' he said, 'it happens whiles with all of us.'

I re-loaded with five in the magazine and one in the breech. As I have said, with a wounded beast you shoot at what you can see, and it can be expensive in ammunition. Then we went across to where the herd had been. They were all out of sight by then, except for the dead beasts lying. My beast's track was a little apart from those of the rest of the running herd, and there was blood on the snow at intervals. Snow makes the tracking of a wounded beast much easier, and this can more than make up for the heavier going. Macandrew looked at the tracks and said, 'She'll go a little and then lie. We'll be up with her soon enough if we go careful.'

I knew this was true. A beast hit too far back will go until she is in cover and then couch, with just her head up, so that you have virtually to stalk her all over again. But you are stalking a beast in a state of full alarm, and the moment she sees you, she will be up and off again. It is a bad, harassing business, and calls for great patience and determination. We went abreast now, because we were both loaded, with the tracks between us, looking for the dark head with the flaring ears which is all we should see of her until she got up again. We went for perhaps a hundred yards, and then Macandrew stopped and pointed. He dropped on one knee and came up into the aim. I still could not see the beast, but the head is not much to see, and even as close to him as I was, I could have been unsighted by the smallest difference in the ground. I got down into a kneeling aim too, ready to fire if the beast showed herself, but for the moment all I could do was to wait for Macandrew. He stayed in the aim for half a minute, and then shook his head and lowered his rifle. I could guess what had happened. The beast was so low to the ground that the mere act of kneeling had unsighted him. He could probably still see the ears, but nothing to shoot at. He got cautiously to his feet, and I did the same, and as we got up, the beast was up and off. Even if either of us had been willing to try a standing shot, she was under a fold in the ground before we could so much as get our rifles up.

We went on again, at least sure of our line, but more cautiously than ever. Even so, the next time we came up with her she saw us before we saw her, and was running again before we knew she was there. This happened twice more, and by that time we must have gone well over half a mile without getting a shot at her. Then we crossed some low ground and came up on to a ridge. The ground fell away steadily in front of us, and there suddenly was our beast in full view, going slowly but determinedly, and all of three hundred yards ahead. I flicked the first leaf of my backsight up and dropped flat on the snow. As I came up into the aim, Macandrew gave a long clear whistle. Just for a moment she hesitated and half turned. I concentrated all I had on the centre of that small dark shape against its huge white background, and when I fired, she dropped where she stood. Macandrew said, 'Yon's good shooting. We'd best go and bring her in to the others.'

I got up, brushing the snow off myself, and uncocked my rifle. The pressure was off now, and my long shot had done something to relieve my misery. I said, 'I hate doing that,' and Macandrew looked at me with his small, quizzical smile and his head a bit on one side.

He said, 'So you should. If you didna feel so, Mr Sinclair would no have you on his ground. There's plenty not so particular.' He looked across to where the beast was lying. 'I tell you what,' he said. 'Do you leave your rifle with me and go and gralloch her and bring her back here. Then maybe I'll give you a hand with her back to the others.'

He sat down comfortably on a rock and pulled out his pipe. I put the Mannlicher muzzle-up on a rock beside him and went off to do my penance. At least I was spared the humiliation of having to look for the beast under his critical eye. The tracks led me straight to her. All the same, it was a long drag back, and by the time we had got all three beasts over the burn and down to the track, even Macandrew was content to call it a day, and it was dark before I got home.

I tried to think constructively about the week-end, but I was dead tired with the cumulative effects of the stresses of two days, and I did not get very far. The one idea I came up with was to wonder if Mary could manage to get out on the Saturday instead of the Sunday, when it was only too likely we should be expected. I could ask her at least. What we had better do when she did get out I still did not know. I told myself that there were two clear days ahead before I need settle anything, and gave it up and went to bed.

The trouble was that the next two days were anything but clear. They were I think the hardest two days we had had since the start, and the Thursday itself was not much better. When I was out on the hill, I could think of nothing but the beasts, and when I got home, I had my usual difficulty in thinking clearly of anything at all. I did come to the view that what we needed above all was to make Davie Bain show his hand, but in circumstances in which he would not have us completely at his mercy. I did not think he would want to show his hand in front of me, but I could not risk letting Mary handle him by herself. Finally I came up with a plan which I thought might meet both difficulties, but there was a lot about it I did not like, and I did not know whether Mary would accept it. At any rate, I could not, conditioned as I was, think of anything better.

I was home soon after five on the Thursday evening, but I should have to go out a bit before six to the tele- phone box at the bridge, and I did not want to get out of my working clothes until I had done that. I cleaned the rifle and pottered about doing various chores while the time moved with dreadful slowness towards six. I was uneasy physically and mentally, and could neither rest nor settle to anything constructive. I longed for a drink, but any drink works powerfully on a tired body and an empty stomach, and I wanted to keep a clear head for my phone call. I went out finally at ten to six. I did not need ten minutes to walk to the box, but I could not stay in the house any longer. As soon as I got outside, the cold struck at me through my clammy clothes, and I walked stiffly with muscles clenched and my skin in a goose-flesh. It was quite dark, but there was a light in the box. I felt suddenly conspicuous standing there in the stale air, but I did not think there would be anyone about, and in any case I might be telephoning anywhere. I got the exchange at five to six, and a moment later Mary came on the line.

I said, 'Look, you couldn't make it Saturday, could you?'

She hesitated for a moment. Then she said, 'Not really. I mean, not in the morning, and we need the whole day pretty well. Why?'

'Only that they'll be expecting us to try again on Sunday. That's on the assumption that they don't know we saw them last time.'

'I see that. But I'm afraid it's a risk we'll have to take.'

I did not know how she was placed at the bank, and I had to accept this. 'All right,' I said. 'Now look. Do you mind doing exactly what you did last Sunday, but doing it alone?'

'Alone?'

'You won't really be alone, not once you get on to Ardevie ground. But I want them to think you are.'

'Where will you be, then?'

'Up on the hill, waiting for you. And for them. I'll come in from this end.'

'You mean, they'll be watching me and you'll be watching them?'

'I'll be watching both of you. I'll be as close up as I can get. I mean, if they move in on you, I'll be there pretty well as soon as they are. But they won't do that until you've got the box, because it's the box they want.' She did not say anything for a moment, and I said, 'Tell me if you can. At the place where the box is, is there clear ground above you? I mean, can you be seen from up on the face?'

'Yes. I know that, because that was why I hid the thing when I did. When I came up out of the forestry, I found myself in full view for a long way round, and I didn't want to be seen carrying it, so I got rid of it as quickly as I could.'

'Good.' I hesitated, and then came out with it. I said, 'You're absolutely sure you can find it?'

She said, 'If there's no more snow. What's it like on the hill now?'

'Almost gone,' I said. 'Only lying in patches.'

'Then that'll be all right if there's no more down.'

'All right,' I said. 'Let's agree on one thing, then. If there's another fall up to Saturday night, don't come at all. If it comes on while you're on the way, turn back at once.'

'What about you, then?'

'If they're there, I'll see them off the ground and then come back here. If they're not, I'll come back at once. But I'll be there to start with, snow or no snow. I want to see them, even if you don't come. If you turn back before the point we reached on Sunday, they won't be interested in you, because they'll know you haven't got it. But the chances are they'll be lying up at about that point, because they'll know the box is somewhere further on.'

She thought about it for a bit. Then she said, 'All right. I agree it makes sense. If they're not there, you'll join me anyhow?'

176

'Of course. But look here, Mary. This is your thing. I'm only suggesting what seems to me the best way of handling it. If you don't like it, say so.'

She said, 'I don't warm to it exactly, but I think you're probably right.'

'It's up to you,' I said.

She said, 'I'll do it.'

'Right. Now one last thing. If for any reason I want you to turn back, snow or no snow, I'll make smoke up on the hill. It'll be somewhere about where we got to on Sunday.'

'You'll do what?'

'Light a fire and raise a column of smoke. It's an old stalkers' trick. You can see it much better than any other sort of signal.'

'I see.'

'So when you get about to the edge of the forestry, keep an eye out for smoke on the hill. Don't do it too obviously. You'll see it all right if it's there. If you see it, just turn back.'

'Why should you need to do that?'

'I don't know. It's just that if there's anything I don't like, and I want to call the thing off, I must have some way of stopping you.'

'Wouldn't they see it?'

'Not very likely. They'll be watching you. I'll be behind them. If I decided to do it, I'd do it only when you were in view, and as soon as I saw you turn back, I'd douse the fire. The chances are they'd never know I'd done it. And the point is, as I've said, that so long as you turn back without reaching the box, you're of no more interest to them. They might not know why you'd turned back, but so long as you had, there'd be nothing more they could do.'

'All right,' she said. 'I've got that. Anything else?'

'Nothing else if you're still determined to get at that

damned box. Think it over between now and Sunday. If you want to get in touch, don't write. I'm not sure it's safe. Better come over than that. Or I could ring you again on Saturday on the chance.'

'No,' she said, 'don't bother. I shan't change my mind. But if anything happens you ought to know about, I'll come over after dark.'

'All right, then. Till Sunday. But if you don't or won't come, don't worry about me. On balance I'd much rather you didn't. But I'll be there anyway.'

We said good-bye and I went out of the box and started to walk home. I was deadly cold now, and had little thought in me but a longing for creature comfort. Above all, I wanted that drink. I told myself I'd think it all over again tomorrow. I could do nothing more tonight.

CHAPTER EIGHTEEN

Friday was another long day, but by the end of it our figures were starting to look better, and Macandrew decided that we should take the Saturday off. However much we changed our ground, the beasts were getting a little wild, and it would do no harm to leave them alone for a couple of days, apart from our own needs. The weather was still cold and grey, with a breeze blowing from anywhere between north-east and nearly full west, but it kept just above freezing, even at night, and the snow was going steadily from the lower ground. On the mountains north and south it was there for the winter, and this helped to make any wind with a bit of north in it colder than it need have been. But I did not think there would be any further fall before the week-end.

I spent the Saturday, as I had the one before, doing my weekly chores. Whatever I had told myself, I did not in fact give much thought to Sunday's plans. I think the truth is that my mind avoided the subject. The thing was agreed now with Mary, and I was afraid of seeing too many flaws in it. In the evening I put out ready all the things I should be taking with me. Some food, my flask, a paraffin fire-lighter of the kind I used to get my wood fires going quickly and my own gas lighter to set it off. In all except soaking weather there is always combustible stuff on the hill, but it can take some starting, and what I should want, if I wanted it at all, was smoke pretty well on the instant. I sealed the fire-lighter in a couple of polythene bags, one inside the other, to keep the smell of it off the food. Lastly I put out a box of cartridges. I do not know quite when I had decided to take the rifle, but I knew now that I would not go without it. It was not only Mr Sinclair's story of the dead man up on Stravachie. God knows, I hoped it would not come to a physical confrontation, but in case it did, I had to have the ultimate argument. As I have said, Davie Bain was a much bigger man than I was, and he might not even be alone. There was nothing to stop me carrying a rifle on Ardevie, even on a Sunday. Sunday shooting is barred by convention, not by law. The only time during the season it is illegal to shoot the beasts is during the hours of darkness, because that is the poachers' time. The beasts come down to the roads at night on their way to the water and the richer feeding in the bottoms, and they have no fear of lights. If anything, they seem to be attracted by them. That is why you hear of poaching gangs from Glasgow and elsewhere working the roads at night with lorries and sub-machine guns. At present prices poaching can be big business. But if I was seen out with a rifle by anyone entitled to be there, though it might not be well regarded, there would be nothing they could do.

I set the alarm for five and went to bed very early. Even when I was in bed I did not worry much about the morning, any more than I had all day. I think the truth is that I had so little idea what I was up against that I should have found it difficult to lie awake thinking about what was going to happen, even if I had wanted to. The one thing I worried about was keeping to my undertaking to Mary. I had to be where I had said I should be before she came along the face from Bunrathie, and I had to be there unbeknownst to anyone else there might be on the hill.

That meant a long walk, most of it in full darkness and all of it well before full daylight, and that meant getting up very early. It was only that I worried about, and that was not enough to keep me awake. I slept in fact quite soon, and was kicked out of deep sleep by the alarm in what felt like the middle of the night.

I put on as many layers of clothing as I could reasonably carry. So far as I knew, I was not likely to be doing anything strenuous enough to make me over-hot, whereas I had the certain prospect of a long lie out in the open, which whatever I wore would make me very cold. I did not feel very hungry, but I ate what I could. I stowed the various things I had to take in my pockets, and took the Mannlicher out of its cupboard and slung it on my shoulder. Then I turned the lights out, and groped my way around in the pitch dark drawing the curtains back from the windows, so that when daylight did come, the place would look reasonably occupied. When I could think of nothing more I ought to do, I let myself out and locked the house behind me.

The sky had cleared considerably, and there were a few stars showing. This would make the first part of my walk a good deal easier, but it also meant that I had to be in position earlier, because I could not risk moving on the hill in any sort of daylight, at least until I knew where everyone else was. If, that is, there was anyone else other than Mary. There was a light breeze from the north-west, and I found myself calculating the effect of this before I realised that it was not the deer I was after. To what I was expecting to stalk, scent meant nothing.

I went down to the road and set out along it eastwards, making all the pace I could. I had decided to walk east to the beginning of the forestry and then south up its western edge, rather than trying to walk direct to its south-west corner. It was two sides of a triangle, but the third side was ground I did not know well, and to negotiate it in full darkness might be a slow and even risky business. By contrast, I could go as fast as my legs would take me on the tarmac, and when I was going straight up the face along the edge of the trees, I should at least be in no doubt about my line, and I was less likely to put a foot seriously wrong. Walking up-hill is always safer, in whatever conditions, than walking across the face. For me to damage myself seriously on this part of the walk would be a disaster I did not dare contemplate.

I did in fact fall once, and fairly heavily, when I was well up the western side of the trees, but I did not hurt myself, and above all managed to keep the rifle from hitting anything that might damage it. I picked myself up and went on, a little out of breath, as you always are after a fall, but thankful it had not been worse. It was still full darkness. There might be the beginnings of daylight in the east by now, but if there were, they were away under the trees, and I could not see them. When I came to the top of the trees, I did turn a few degrees eastward, but mainly I kept on climbing. It was height I wanted now. Once I was high enough up the face, I could adjust my position east or west when the daylight showed up the trees below me, but for the moment my main consideration was to get well across the line anyone approaching from the east was likely to come in on.

The skies were paler now, ahead of me and on my left hand, and presently I knew I could see the skyline above me, not as a mere absence of stars, but as a curved line of solid darkness against the growing grey behind it. Behind me in the glen I could still see nothing, and it was very difficult to tell how high up the face I now was. But on mere dead reckoning I thought I must be as high as I was likely to want, and I flattened my line still further, until I was moving almost eastward along the face. The ground began to take shape round me now as I moved, and the next time I stopped and looked down, I could see a faint pattern of light and dark in the bottom of the glen and against it the dark line which I knew was the trees fringing the slope of the hill. It was well down, and as far as I could see came to its eastern end almost directly below me. I had finished the main part of my walk, and it was time I stopped and took stock. When I could see more, I could decide on my final position, but for the moment I could do no good by moving. I found a small hollow between two rocks and sat down in it, with my head just clear of their tops, to wait for daylight.

My position, when I found it, must of course be one from which I could see Mary when in due course she came along the lower ground to the eastern end of the trees. But it would not be Mary I was watching for. I knew exactly where she would appear, and I knew roughly when, and that would not be for some time yet. In the meantime I had to watch for someone who might or might not come, I did not know when or where from, though I thought he would come from the east and on a line higher than Mary's but still below me. Once there was any real daylight this should not be too difficult, because any movement catches the eye on the hill, where nothing else moves at all. But daylight I must have, and daylight is a thing you can only wait for. So I sat and waited for the daylight and for a man, both from the east, and the man came, and from the east, but before the daylight.

I should not have seen him at all but for the deer, and I should not have seen him then if he had come below me, but he came above me, and I saw him for a moment against the grey of the sky. I do not know how long I had been sitting there when I heard the deer. I heard them running east of me and a little up-hill, and then, quite near at hand, I heard them snort, and a moment later I

183

saw them, just their heads in silhouette against the sky, perhaps a dozen of them, running up-hill and away from me, towards the south-west. I knew what had happened. I knew they had been running westwards along the face, and had run into my scent, and switched their line away from me up the hill. That would have been when I heard the snorts. The leading beast would have picked up my scent and snorted and shied away from it, and the rest would have followed her. But I knew I was not the one that had made them run. Whatever had made them run had come up to them suddenly in the half-light from down-wind, and if it had done that, it was coming my way. I crouched there between the rocks, with just the top of my head up, and waited for whatever it was to show itself. I waited for perhaps a couple of minutes, and then it came.

It was a man, with just the top half of him against the skyline, going steadily and stealthily westwards. It was my picture of the hunting man. The deer would have known him, Sunday or no Sunday. No wonder they ran. But I did not think it was the deer he was after. I saw him only for a moment, but there was something straight in a diagonal line across his body, as if he had a stick under his arm. Only I did not think it was a stick. If a man has a stick on the hill, he carries it in his hand, not under the crook of his arm. Then he was out of sight, going westwards and slightly northwards. I thought I knew where he was making for. I did not move a muscle, but let him go.

I knew what I had to do. I had to stop Mary. If there were two men with guns on the hill, whatever they had in their minds, the hill was no place for her. But I could not stop her from here. I was still well above the sort of place I had intended to lie up in and wait for her, and I did not command an uninterrupted view of her line, as I should need to do if I was going to make sure of her seeing the smoke. I considered the possibility of making off eastwards and trying to cut her off, but it would be too easy to miss her. I could not be sure of getting on to the line we had come by before, nor could I be certain, if I did, that she would come by it. Indeed, knowing her and her caution, I thought it very likely she would not. The only place I knew she had to come by was the north-eastern corner of the trees, and that would be in full view of whoever was watching on the hill. So I kept to the agreed plan of making smoke, only I had to get down to the right place to do it, and I had to get there without being seen from further along the hill. And it was getting lighter all the time.

It took me a long time, but I managed it. In view of what happened later, I know I must have managed it. I crawled at last into a hollow facing northwards, which commanded a good view of the lower ground, but was just unsighted from further west along the face. I did not know how much time I had left, but I did not think it could be very much. It took me some time to collect the dry heather tops for my fire, because I had to crawl to get them, but finally I reckoned I had enough. I was piling them up on the lip of the hollow, with the fire-lighter under them, when I saw Mary. She was earlier than I had expected and much nearer. I think she must have come up from the lower ground eastward of the forestry, because she appeared quite suddenly only thirty yards or so from the corner of the trees. She looked a tiny figure at that distance, but there was no mistaking her. I put the finishing touches to my fire, and put my hand in my breeches pocket for the gas lighter, and found it was not there.

For a second or two my mind stopped working altogether. I expect I went through the instinctive, idiot motions of feeling my other pockets, but I knew it was not there either. I knew where it had been, but it must have slipped out when I fell. I looked at the piled-up kindling, as if there must be some way of putting fire to it, but of course there was none. And all the time Mary was passing steadily across my field of vision down at the bottom of the hill. I saw her glance up for a moment, and I jumped to my feet and waved frantically, but she had turned her head again before I was up, and in any case she would almost certainly not have seen me. You see only what you are looking for on the hill, and she was looking for smoke, not a minute gesticulating figure dark against a neutral background. The next moment it was too late. She had moved on westward, and I picked up my rifle and went westward after her. But before I went, I pushed five cartridges into the magazine of the Mannlicher and brought the bolt forward over them. I did not know what I should want with a loaded rifle, but an unloaded rifle is as useless as a broken stick.

I knew my man was westwards of me, and I hoped he was still below me, but until I had got him placed, I had to go very carefully indeed. I thought he would be at the place where I had seen movement the Sunday before, but if I tried to find that place from above, I should be lucky if I got within several hundred yards of it. The only thing to do was to see him, and I was most likely to see him when he moved. I thought he would move, because I thought he would be above the point where we had turned back last week, and when Mary went on beyond that, he would be bound to move along with her. I thought that once I had got him placed, the three of us would move along the face in parallel, Mary just above the top of the trees, my man perhaps a hundred and fifty yards above her and myself the same distance above him. He would be watching Mary, and I should be watching both of them. I did not know at all what would come of it, but the operation itself should not be too difficult. Only I had to find him first.

I went westward and slightly upward, spying over every inch of the ground ahead before I made any move. I did not know how far west he was or what sort of position he would have taken up, but I was confident that unless I did something to attract his attention, he would not be looking in my direction. Unless I walked right on top of him, I had every chance of seeing him first. In the end I saw him, as I had thought I might, when he moved. He got up suddenly out of the heather about a hundred yards below me and a little ahead. I saw what he had in his hands all right. He hesitated for a moment, and then crouched and moved off westwards. He did not look either up or down the face, but hurried westwards as if time was very much his concern. I knew what was worrying him, and it worried me too. The face of the hill was convex here. I had lost sight of Mary altogether, and I thought he had too. All the same, I did not move as long as he was moving, because then there was nothing to fix his attention, and if for any reason he did turn round when I was on my feet, the chances were that he would see me, however quick I was to drop. Instead, I let him go as far as he wanted, until finally he turned and crawled out on to the shoulder of the slope, and lay there, looking down the hill again. From the angle of his head, it looked as if he had caught up with Mary again, and she was now directly below him.

As soon as he was settled, I moved. I moved as fast as I could, watching him all the time in case he looked like getting ready to move on again. I knew that when he had to move, he would slide backwards a yard or two before he went on with his westward movement, and this would give me time to get under cover. In fact he did just that, but not until I had gained a lot of ground on him. I was

187

still not directly above him, but I had not much more distance to make up. He moved twice more, and each time as soon as he stopped moving, I moved after him. I was moving gradually downhill too, so that the whole time the distance between us was closing. Stalking a man is likely to be more important than stalking the deer, but it is certainly a lot easier. Not only have you not got that tremendous battery of senses to contend with, but a man's mind focuses his attention in whatever direction he is interested in, whereas the deer, with one sense or another, keep all the ground covered all the time.

The third time I moved I actually got ahead of him, and now suddenly the ground below me fell away, and I could see Mary again. She was going slower now, and I thought more hesitantly, looking about her. Also, I real-ised that my man had been moving downwards, closing in on her just as I was closing in on him, until now she was hardly a hundred and fifty yards below me, with him about half-way between us. The next time he moved, he moved to a point directly below me, and when I looked at her, I saw that Mary had stopped too. We stopped there, all three of us, in an almost straight line down the face and perhaps sixty yards apart. He lay flat on the heather looking down at her, so that I could see the hump of his head and shoulders against the dark background of the trees. I lay similarly above him, but no one saw me, because no one looked. Then Mary moved.

She moved a few yards to the left and knelt and began working at something on the ground. I watched her, holding my breath, and then suddenly she stood up, and I saw that she was holding something small and square in her hands. I do not know what made me do it, but I took my eyes off her and looked at the man below me and saw that he was up in the aim.

I think I tried to shout, but my voice did not come.

Instead I flung my rifle up, working the bolt as I brought the butt into my shoulder. For a split second I steadied the sights on that humped figure on the face below me, and then I fired. I saw his head jerk back and fall forward, and the muzzle of his rifle tilted sharply upwards, as if he had fallen forward over the stock. But I knew, even as I saw it, that he had fired first. I looked for Mary, but could not see her anywhere. I got up and began running down the face. My voice had come back to me, and I shouted as I ran, but no one answered me and nothing moved.

I did not go near Davie Bain at all. I ran straight down to where I thought Mary had been, and I could not find her. That was the awful thing. I knew she was there somewhere, but I could not see her. It was a nightmare repetition of the familiar difficulty of finding your fallen beast, and without thinking about it I went automatically into the familiar routine, casting round in wider and wider circles round the place where I had expected to find her. I came on her quite suddenly, as you do. She was lying spread-eagled over a flat rock, just as I had seen her in my mind's eye spreadeagled over a stone in the graveyard of the Maceacherns, and she looked just as small as I had imagined she would.

I knew she was dead from the way she lay. Take the mind out, and all bodies behave much the same. Davie Bain had had a much better target than I had had, and he was no doubt just as good a shot. The box lay a yard away from her, upside down, but with the lid half open. I do not know whether she had been opening it or whether it had hit a rock and broken itself open as it fell. I went over to it and turned it over with my foot. I do not know what I expected, I suppose jewellery of some sort, but only one thing fell out, a single heavy thing wrapped in an oily rag. I hardly needed to touch it to know what it was. It was a gun, an automatic pistol of some sort. I did not unwrap it. I thought I could guess part of its history, and I knew that in the wrong hands it must have been life and death to Davie Bain. The police would know, too. The only thing left was to get the whole business into their hands as soon as possible. My own position I did not consider. I was conscious of no wrong-doing, only of one enormous error of judgement made lethal by one small incalculable accident. I did not know what the law would say.

I took my jacket off and spread it over Mary. At full stretch it covered almost the whole of her. Then I spread heather-tops on the jacket, to distract the attention of predators. I left Davie Bain as he was. I hitched the Mannlicher over my shoulder and set off down the hill. It was easier going now, but I did not know how long it would take me to reach the telephone box.